D1076101

BESTSELLER

Muir took leave from his White House post to write a biography of Roger Liversedge, the United States' first black Vice President. Muir didn't expect his book to sell particularly well, but then fate took a hand — President Henry Roberts suffered a fatal heart attack and Liversedge was sworn in as President. As Muir watched the helicopter arrive at the White House with the new President on board there was a huge flash — Liversedge had been assassinated, and within two hours Muir's biography was a bestseller!

RUSSELL WARREN HOWE

BESTSELLER

Complete and Unabridged

LINFORD
Leicester

First published in the
United States of America

First Linford Edition
published 2001

British Library CIP Data

Howe, Russell Warren, *1925* –
    Bestseller.—Large print ed.—
    Linford mystery library
    1. Detective and mystery stories
    2. Large type books
    I. Title
    823.9'14 [F]

    ISBN 0–7089–5927–X

Published by
F. A. Thorpe (Publishing)
Anstey, Leicestershire

Set by Words & Graphics Ltd.
Anstey, Leicestershire
Printed and bound in Great Britain by
T. J. International Ltd., Padstow, Cornwall

This book is printed on acid-free paper

For Hallowell Bowser,
in memoriam

Author's Note

Bestseller was written in 1979. The events are projected to have taken place in 1983, which would have been the next to last year of the fortieth United States Presidency. Obviously, President Roberts and Vice President Liversedge bear no relation whatsoever to President Reagan and Vice President Bush, who were to be in office at that time.

Part One

The Night That Everyone Remembers

1

If he had known that Barry Remington would be at Chez Solange, a Vietnamese restaurant near Key Bridge, Muir would have gone to lunch at any of a score of different Georgetown places. It was not that he disliked Remington's company. Remington was the diplomatic correspondent of one of the networks, a pleasant, handsome, smooth reporter, a junior-avuncular forty-year-old who could recount a revolution or a summit conference in thirty seconds. For this small but marketable skill, Remington made nearly twice as much as the Secretary of State he covered, and Muir respected that. But finding Remington alone, and being alone himself, meant that Muir was virtually obliged to share his colleague's table, once Remington invited him, and that meant talking shop. It was a clear, sunny, June day in Washington, but it was not one of Muir's

3

good days, and he did not feel like talking about the crafts of writing or reporting.

A pretty Eurasian waitress in an *ao dai* fluttered into their company and took Muir's order, then hopped away, settling like an exotic moth at another table. Remington said: 'When are you going back to real work?'

'In four months, I guess,' Muir said.

'I envy you your year off. How's the book going?'

'Nearly finished,' said Muir. That was true; what was also true was that the book was the reason he did not feel like discussing writing.

'You'll take over from Brad Williams — ' Remington interrupted himself and thrust his shoulders back to make room for a tray of *cha gio* ordered earlier.

'In October.'

The two men nodded their thanks at the waitress. Then, Remington clutched a *cha gio* firmly in a pair of chopsticks and twisted it in a shallow bowl of *nuoc mam* and red pepper. Muir followed suit.

'You think you'll like covering the White House?' The question sounded trite, but Remington showed no surprise at Muir's answer.

'I think I'll hate it.'

'I think it would be worse than the State Department,' Remington agreed.

The two of them went back to eating *cha gio* in their crackling, rice-flour wrappers. But with Remington, all conversation tended to degenerate into an interview. After a sip of jasmin tea, he had another question.

'When does the book appear?'

'In eighteen months — when Liversedge leaves office.'

Remington stretched his napkin against his lips to absorb the tea remaining there, and stared at the people at the next table. Then he focused on Muir again.

'You have any trouble getting the year off? They do that sort of thing at the *Post* all the time, but you don't hear of it with the chains. If I took even six months off, I'd be finished. The brass would say that people had forgotten my face. In any event, I have other plans.'

Muir didn't ask him what they were; he was not interviewing Remington.

'Trouble? No,' he heard himself saying, 'Smith Newspapers is a pretty good outfit on the whole. Duane Smith only barely made it through Kansas State, and he wouldn't know an ellipsis from a metaphor, but I think he means it when he says that he likes to cultivate his writers.'

'Who took over from you as their investigative reporter?'

'Ferdy Stein.'

'And Brad Williams retires in October?'

'Right.'

The exotic moth alighted once more; her naive smile raised the hint of a lusty look in Remington's eye. A silvery platter of *my sao* appeared between them. Remington said: 'I heard you had to go all the way to Kansas City to talk him into giving you a sabbatical.'

Muir wondered why reporters gossiped so much about other reporters. He said: 'Smith asked me to go down there to offer me Williams' job, and to give me a year or so's notice that it was coming up, and also so I could talk about the Roberts era in Washington to a head-office staff dinner. He said he thought the book on Liversedge was a good idea.'

'And he offered you that part-time radio spot at the same time? I like your program, by the way.' He napkined his lips again.

'Thanks. No, that was my idea, and Steve Morton's — he's the program manager. It forces me to keep in touch and it provides a little beer money. The chain owns the station, of course.'

'I know. That reminds me,' said Remington, looking up appealingly as the waitress wafted by again, 'could we have a carafe of dry white wine?'

They ate for a moment in silence until it came. Remington poured it carefully into the two glasses, then looked at his own against the light as though the contents might prove to be of a worthy vintage. He sipped, then said: 'I understand how you feel. Do you realize how long I've done the State Department?'

'Seven years? Eight?'

'Nearly ten. And what do I have to look forward to? The White House job? Perhaps with a little extra money, to make

7

it appear to be promotion?' His normally serious features looked boyish as he became more confidential. He went on: 'And even then, what next? My chances of becoming Uncle Barry and reading the network news in New York are slim at best, and there's nothing really attractive about that eunuch post, to a journalist, except the obscene salary. I could end up doing the State Department for *thirty years*!'

'So you're going to write another book, and damn the consequences,' Muir said.

'No. I'm going to run for the U.S. Senate.'

Muir's chopsticks stopped a centimeter short of his lips as he tried to judge whether Remington was serious. He responded with a flip remark.

'It would mean a drop in salary.'

Remington wasn't listening. 'I've got face and name recognition. I've got a voice that audiences like. Why not?'

Remington lived in Bethesda, just beyond the District line, so that presumably meant he would be thinking of contesting in Maryland. 'There must be other contenders,' Muir said. 'Or are you running as a Republican, and no-one else wants to run against an incumbent?'

The two current Maryland senators came from both parties. The Republican, Matthews, was up for re-election the following year.

'I'm a Democrat,' said Remington. Muir found it hard to think of any colleague as party-oriented. 'I'd be going after Matthews' seat. Bob Wilson, the black congressman in Baltimore, wants the nomination and he has a lot of the machine behind him. But race would be a factor.'

'In the primaries, you'd bomb him on the Eastern Shore. Would you want to win because you're white?'

'I sure wouldn't, but what's the choice?' Remington asked. 'Politics is politics.'

Muir loaded his half-empty ricebowl with a generous helping of *my sao*, chopsticked some into his mouth and put down the bowl. He drank some wine. He was glad the conversation had shifted from himself to Remington.

'Barry, I just don't see you talking to housewives in the supermarket. What do you know about fishermen's problems, or land-zoning in Anne Arundel County?'

'What did I know about Afghanistan? What does Bob Wilson know about the fiduciary mechanics of the Federal Reserve? Senators, and candidates for senator, have researchers, too, more of them than I have now.'

Muir shook his head. 'There are a lot of phonies in our business, Barry, but it's a big field and you don't meet all the players every day. There are only a hundred senators. I've heard you going on about the Hill phonies over the years, the Ted Kennedys, the Frank Churches, the Scoop Jacksons. You'd be dealing with guys like that all the time.'

'It's a game, Don. It's theater.'

'But in theater,' said Muir, 'you know who the bad guys are. They even know it themselves. But we're talking about people who fool people. They even fool their wives and children.'

Remington said defensively: 'Why don't you do a piece or a radio segment in which you analyze a week in Congress as though you were the *Times* drama critic? I can hear it now: Senator Spook wasn't quite as effective this time as the good guy with the heart of dross, but his strengthening amendments to the Anti-Famine Bill enabled him to deliver a remarkable soliloquy to an almost empty chamber, flourishing photographs of starving infants.'

'It's certainly not an impossible thought, running for the Senate,' Muir conceded vaguely. 'I guess my first reaction was personal, that I wouldn't want the job myself.'

Remington seemed pleased to find a reason for probing Muir again. 'Well, what *are* you going to do?'

'I might write a novel.'

'I got to thinking about writing a novel, in 1980, during the Democratic Convention,' Remington said. 'Not about how A triumphed and B got shafted, that's non-fiction, but something more human. One idea I had was a sort of Sanford-and-son couple who get the contract to clean up the muck after each day's performance, and who find all sorts of sellable things on the floor — a gold watch, an incriminating letter, a medical prescription showing that an ambitious politician is dying of an obscure Tibetan disease. My agent said it wasn't sexy enough.'

Remington was grinning boyishly as he went on: 'So I thought of this story about a Manhattan secretary whom nobody takes seriously. Her husband doesn't take her seriously, her lover doesn't take her seriously, her boss thinks she's just a gorgeous nitwit whom it's fun to steal away with to business meetings in Des Moines. So she quarrels with her husband, stands her boyfriend up on a date, and goes off to dinner alone in a restaurant. She orders *chateaubriant* with braised endives and the waiter brings her rockfish and peas.

'When she tells him to take it back he tells her *she* made the mistake, not him. That does it! Somebody has got to take her seriously! The next day she buys a gun and in the evening she goes to the Convention to shoot the nominee at the moment his delegate count goes over the magic figure.

'But while she's waiting there in the crowd, she gets to thinking that she's not being original enough to be taken seriously. Lee Harvey Oswald killed Kennedy so that his wife would take him seriously. Arty Bremer shot Governor Thingumy from Alabama to hit the front pages, and so on.

'So she lets the guy get nominated and then, when he's at the rhetorical heights of his acceptance speech, and there isn't a dry eye in the hall, she takes off all her clothes and walks down the center aisle smoking a fat cigar.'

Remington was beginning to giggle at his own undergraduate humor, and Muir found it infectious. Both men laughed to ease their tensions, then fell back to eating and drinking and to forgetting for a moment what they had been talking about.

After a while, the smile lines receded from Remington's features. He said: 'So what's next for you? You grow bored and jaded in the White House, running after

Roberts and his successors like some three-piece-suited beggar seeking alms? With your handle on Liversedge, why don't you go for an ambassadorship?'

Muir smiled. 'I've always wanted to spend some time in Mauritius,' he said. He was talking off the top of his head. 'That was one place I never got to.'

'Mauritius, hell!' said Remington. 'Through Liversedge, you could have Rome, or Athens as a fall-back demand.'

'Demand?'

'Sure. All you're getting out of this relationship with Liversedge is a book about a vice president. That's a noble effort, but then what?'

Remington's mention of Rome and Athens had set Muir to thinking of the Mediterranean.

'I don't think I'd want to run a great diplomatic factory. Malta might be interesting. Or maybe not an ambassadorship, but the Peace Corps. It might be nice to run the Peace Corps mission in Tuvalu, if they have one there.'

'Where?'

'Tuvalu. It's a group of Pacific islands

with about ten thousand people, but it's independent.'

Remington looked at him with a glance that suggested disappointment, even disapproval. Clearly, running a small bank of latterday American hippies on the U.S. payroll in Gauguinland didn't measure up, in Remington's eyes, to being a United States senator. There was a moment's silence. Muir ate the last of his *my sao*, and as he put the bowl down the thoughts of Tuvalu and Mauritius went along with it. They became like the scraps of discarded rice on the flat plate around the bowl. He had only been engaging in conversation, not making plans.

★ ★ ★

As Muir came out later from under the overpass on K, leaving the Georgetown waterfront, and walked toward Thompson's Boatyard, he saw the sun glinting on the Arlington Memorial Bridge; he saw its rays mirrored again in the tall black glass of the Rosslyn skyline, looming over the trees on the Virginia side of the placid river. There had been a time when such visions had improved his day. He asked himself if he wasn't spending too much time cocooned, if he didn't perhaps miss the constant discipline of being conscripted to Today's Event. But he had tried to convince himself of that, often before, and failed.

A 737 went through the arc of its final, its nose centered on midriver; the nose lifted gently, and the aircraft began its ultimate pancake into National. There was an air of smooth inevitability about a landing plane: You knew exactly what it was going to do. Muir watched it to clear his mind.

When he had taken the year's unpaid leave to write the biography of Roger Liversedge, the first black vice president of the United States, it had been with the brash hope of writing a bestseller, of establishing himself as independently self-employed, and with turning down — or resigning in short order from — the White House post. This was, he knew, a goal he shared with many colleagues, including of course Remington, whose anecdotal book about traveling with Brzezinski, a few years before, had sold only about four thousand copies in hard cover. (The Senate, Muir suspected, had been Remington's second choice, selected when his book about Brzezinski had failed and his pipedream about a novel had evaporated.) Now it seemed clear that Muir would not be able to break out of pattern so easily. His book, he believed, was not going to do much better than Remington's, and the notion of an ambassadorship seemed even more absurd than it had seemed at lunch. Soon, he would be just one of the quirky journalistic jesters at the overpopulated court of President Henry Roberts — then, after that, a part of whatever overpopulated White House court came next. Roberts had had a mild heart attack and had announced that he would retire after a single term. For a decade or two, Muir would be tied to each new president's whims and travels; he would learn to resent the long, rather narrow press room in the low West Wing; when he journeyed abroad with the President, he would envy the foreign correspondents who would really know what was going on in the places where he would know only what the President did while he was there. His life would be locked into daily deadlines, to cultivating the self-important sources whose names were so easily forgotten one administration later, to seeing day by day the same competitors-colleagues-friends. To talking shop, endlessly.

Muir delayed going home, walking instead through the parking lot of Thompson's Boatyard and on to the wide cement jetty. Two muscled men went through the exercise of handling a racing scull into the water, locking oars into outriggers, balancing themselves into place on the traction seats, slipping their feet into the clamps, gingerly edging off into the stream with their port oars, the starboard oars resting on the water to give them balance.

There had been a time when membership of the pack had been a source of pleasure. But that had been overseas, where the pack was a pack of dissidents, of lone rangers who came together only for protection and relaxation and to share the privilege of being five thousand miles from what was called the cable desk. In all, he had reported from sixty-three countries and lived in nine. Now, two of his three foreign languages were rusting, used only occasionally at diplomatic receptions. At least, with Vuissane, he could still speak French. But it had been at his own misguided request that the chain had brought him home, ten years before, to fill the newly created post of chief investigative reporter in Washington. The post itself was a fad of the times, but it earned a lot of front-page space. And this had led, inexorably, to Smith, over sole in a French restaurant in Kansas City, saying that Williams planned to retire and 'I presume you would like his job.'

It had certainly not been an unnatural presumption. Having a journalistic talking part in the Chinese opera of the White House was a sort of imprimatur on a reporter's career. Other stories were often more interesting and usually more challenging, but the White House was the Vatican of temporal power. The tired, rather bloated features of Henry Roberts, former senior senator from Indiana, fortieth president of the United States, composed the face that launched a thousand crises and counter-crises around the world. He was the reporter's certain passport to unlimited space, to a byline that even readers, not just other journalists, recognized.

Muir sat on a bench and watched a sculler racing past toward the Georgetown University yard, and he thought about his mediocre book which was now turtling toward a finish. Roger Liversedge had certainly been a natural subject. He and Muir had been at high school together in Queenston, Rhode Island, during Liversedge's last year there — the future Vice President had been two years older. They had been contemporaries for two years at Brown. They had kept in contact for nearly thirty years after that, as Muir trotted the globe and as Liversedge had risen from the D.A.'s office in Providence to vice chairman of the state Democratic Party, to the state attorney-generalship, and finally, after a hectic six-candidate primary, to Governor.

But Liversedge's qualities did not help the book. He was, in his public life, a reserved, rather patrician figure. His father, a Unitarian minister, had been the head of Queenston's only black family. Liversedge had been, in effect, an honorary white who was only really black when it suited him. He had not had to fight to be Vice President. He had been Roberts' choice: The big, shambling, pushy Indianan had wanted what the ultra-conservative Manchester *Union-Leader* had tartly called an Arthur Treacher; hiring a black one had helped Roberts collar an elusive liberal vote, tempted by the first left-of-center Republican selected by his party for the presidency for over a generation.

In the job, Liversedge had been almost blameless, taking on more and more foreign-affairs chores in the Third World, where most of the challenging diplomacy was now conducted, and where an eggshell-colored, stocky six-footer with an old-fashioned clipped mustache and a quiet voice had been easily accepted. Muir had enjoyed easy access to Liversedge, and the book would include a number of revelations about the hard infighting that had gone on in countless international negotiations. One, in particular, would be momentous. But Muir's desire to write the book had stemmed less from the fact that he liked the subject personally and knew him better than any other reporter did, than because he saw the book as a step toward liberation; now it looked as though it would only be a short parole. On balance, the ten-to-twelve, week-night radio show — chatter on 'national, international and human affairs', and music, mostly classical jazz — had proved more rewarding than the book.

★   ★   ★

A small commuter plane buzzed over-head, arcing into National. Muir imagined the pilot staring down the runway, the only place where he could go.

Muir glanced at the masthead of a *Post* lying on the bench and reread the date: June 20, 1983. Only three and three quarter months of his parole remained. He was fifty-three, an age, it seemed, for crucial decisions, and he found himself virtually paralyzed by a desire not to make any. He was still awaiting a sort of Islamic predestination, like a trucker betting the state lottery every week and assuming that, if he was 'good', a lucky number would take decisions out of his hands.

Writing the book had posed no special problems except Muir's own difficulties in organizing what for him was a great deal of material: perhaps a hundred thousand words, no more — but his first book. It was a different discipline from his own, and one for which he now realized he had no real training, only a virtual obligation to finish somehow. Liversedge had been endlessly accommodating. But most of his life, inspected in detail, had never been momentous, except for its *Ebony* quality — the first black this, the only black that. Liversedge had positioned himself well at each crucial step in his career; but set out in endless paragraphs, it looked like the wheeling and dealing of any political life story. Which was exactly what it had been. There had been no great tragedies, and no romance. Liversedge had never married. His few female relationships had been discreet, seemingly almost platonic, mostly with foreign women, particularly orientals. He seemed emotionally almost neuter. He had been suspected, wrongly so far as Muir could determine, of homosexuality. He was a man who exerted a strong will with great politeness, and who rarely opened his mouth at all on anything significant until the thought was not only chewed but almost pre-digested. More spontaneous people were irritated by his caution. He was a self-prepackaged politician, and you had to listen to his jokes and his anecdotes to realize that he was not only human but humane. Liversedge, Muir had decided, knew more, much more, about others, than anyone, including Muir, would ever really learn about the pastor's son.

Certainly, the book went over, in detail, ground that had been barely scratched in articles and news stories. There had been recollections of a disciplined childhood, tales of school and college, his brush with death during an enemy air strike in Korea — a war which he had spent, unadventurously, in the Judge-Advocate's Office, mostly defending deserters — and memoirs of no surpassing originality about brief conversations with such droppable names as Jack Kennedy, Hubert Humphrey, Martin Luther King, Bob Haldeman and Jimmy Carter. Liversedge had wisely refused the ambassadorship in Stockholm which Nixon had offered him: Not that diplomatic service in the Nixon administration would have been held against him in the party, given his color, but because it would have taken him out of contention for the governorship. He had started as only third favorite in the primary, as it was, and his election had been a judicious compromise worked out by party regulars and the

Portuguese-American bloc from the two counties on the eastern shore of the Sakonnet. The most interesting material really lay in his international negotiations, but even these did not seem enough to put the book on the top-ten list of the New York *Times*. For over a decade now, the American public had had a surfeit of revealed political drama; the currency of such entertainment had been debased.

With most of the draft written, Muir was already afraid that the book would be, like Remington's, just another of Washington's endless political titles, relying for its uniqueness almost entirely on the fact that Liversedge was about one-quarter African in descent. It would sell, no doubt, like hot cakes in Rhode Island; but Rhode Island wasn't exactly California. Indeed, one of the problems of the book as Muir, a foreign correspondent by vocation, saw it, was the very parochialness of Liversedge's life: Except for vacations, occasional trips to New York and the capital, and the youthful interlude in Korea immediately after college, Roger had been virtually nowhere outside his home state until he became Vice President and began his attorney-like missions to foreign countries.

Muir was sufficiently depressed about the Liversedge biography to have done no work on it at all for the past two days. That afternoon, he decided, when he had finished some guideline material for the evening show, he would, with what time remained, try to complete Chapter Twelve, the next-to-last.

Muir wished, as he had done often in recent months, that there had been some dark scandal in the Vice President's life, or at least a real conflict with the party somewhere; even his ethnic label seemed to have helped rather than hindered him, as Liversedge had profited from the frantic search for black talent in the Sixties and Seventies. There had been accusations, many years ago, in a Newport weekly, that he had been bribed, as D.A., to drop a case against a local Mafia figure. But Liversedge had weathered that charge successfully; the figure had fortuitously died shortly afterward; and Muir had only Liversedge's account to go by — the Newport editor, now living in retirement in Acapulco, had refused to answer Muir's letters. Even if there had been some great romantic chapter in Liversedge's history, Muir reflected, it would probably only have interested black readers.

Could the book be saved? Liversedge had made it clear, three years before, at the party convention, that he would never 'go for any higher office.' This had been the price of his getting the vice-presidential nomination. The country was not yet ready for a black president, even a Republican one — unless, perhaps, the Democrats ran a retired marine general or a woman with a New York accent. The fact that Roberts was not running for re-election the following year would put Liversedge out to pasture even sooner than had been expected. It had led to Liversedge being even more forthcoming, on the understanding that the book would only appear just after he left office. I am writing, Muir reminded himself, a book about a man who will be a *former* vice president by the time it appears. How many Americans even remembered the names of their former vice presidents? He wished that he had chosen to write about something else, something that would hit the charts.

Back at the Watergate, the Yoruba clerk on duty at the front desk handed Muir a message, to call Vuissane. He did so as soon as he reached his apartment. Ten minutes later, he was at her place, two floors down, under the sheets, and holding her close to him.

2

At times like this, they never talked much, and what they had to say was said in French because Muir's French was better than her English, and she was always more relaxed in her own language; he for his part instinctively felt that, in talking French, his emotional life was switched to a different plane from all the rest. It was a different box, separate from the boxes that were less rewarding — the book, his boredom with his career, and the countless irritations which you developed in a half-century or so of living, one of which was a failed former marriage where the language of love had also been the language of everything else.

'I needed you,' Vuissane said.

'Good.'

His lips began to travel over her body, gaining pleasure from giving pleasure. She responded with caresses and occasional drawings-in of breath. Then she gently pushed his shoulders back and began to respond: The mouth with which she sang became an instrument of silent expression, making him aware of almost nothing but her. Her guitar, he noticed, was in its usual place in a corner, resting against a woven Algerian curtain; but for the moment it was no more a part of anything to do with life outside than if it had been his typewriter or the thermostat; it was only part of Vuissane's setting, the comfortably familiar backdrop to their private reality which the outside world was not meant to touch. Only, a little later, when her sighs of climax seemed to come from the furthest reaches of her throat did it sound to him like her music, and he was reminded that he had fallen in love with her voice before anything else — that the infatuation which had matured until it became a sort of symphonic leitmotif that compensated for the gross cacophony of daily life was related to her plaintive verses.

Afterward, she lay with her head on his chest, her long hair covering her face and her shoulders like a silken shawl. They

31

indulged in the fruits of silence.

He had never asked Vuissane her age. It had always seemed as irrelevant as those wasted spaces in news stories which told you how many years had passed since a burglar or a cabinet officer was born — an American quirk which Muir had rediscovered when he returned home from overseas. But Vuissane had talked offhandedly, a few days before, about moving in with him, and the practical thought now occurred to Muir that she would probably outlive him; he felt selfishly sorry for her, *la veuve* Muir. She was, he guessed, about twenty-six, if you took it from the year when she had graduated from Grenoble and the length of her first marriage and the brief extent of her career.

Vuissane was a folk singer; her audience did not usually understand her words, except when she sang at the French Embassy soirées; but her deep, slightly artificially husky voice was well known on the Washington night bar scene. Only the Immigration people, the retired doctor in Florida who owned her Watergate apartment, Muir and a few others knew her family name; she had introduced to Washington the French stage vanity of using only her given name — in her case, a rare medieval one chosen by her father, a professor of pre-sixteenth century literature at the Sorbonne.

'Guess where I'm going?' Her whisper was followed by a yawn.

'When?' His eyes were closed.

'Today.'

'No idea.'

He opened his eyes to find Vuissane smiling childishly.

'To the White House,' she said.

'You're singing tonight?'

'No. It's my free day.'

'I mean at the White House.'

'No. I'm coaching the President in French.'

President Roberts was leaving for Paris at the weekend. He had had to come down from the Camp David talks to prepare. Muir had read somewhere that he planned to make his Elysée banquet speech in French.

'You? Why not the State Department people?'

'Someone in his office called. That time I sang at the White House, when he was entertaining the Cambodian — president? prime minister? remember? — he said he enjoyed my songs, and he'd like to have me visit the White House privately one day. The woman in his office said he wanted me to go through his speech with him tonight at seven o'clock and correct his pronunciation.'

'The old rascal. That's nice of him.'

'I'm glad about it. It's — special. I have heard you say, it's not what you know but who you know. Well, now I will know the President. That should help me with my labor permit.'

Muir sleepily murmured his approval and drifted off. She must have slept also, because when he opened his eyes again the inner courtyard of the Watergate outside the window was full of shadow. She was groping across him for his watch, on a table on his side of the bed.

'Five-thirty,' she said.

'What time did you say you had to be

there? Seven o'clock?'

'From seven to eight. I must be on time.' She sat up.

He stretched, rubbed his eyes, clasped his hands behind his head to peer at the shadowed wall of apartments across the courtyard.

'You have an hour and a half. A lifetime.'

★　★　★

Through the slightly open bathroom door, he could see her combing her waistlength hair, tossing her head. He watched her wash and splash eau de cologne on her suntanned body. She made the usual helpless push at the door, which was swollen and would never quite close, then sat on the toilet.

'Regard elsewhere, pig!'

The pig grinned from his pillow, declining to regard elsewhere.

With theatrical dressing-room speed, Vuissane was ready. She wore no make-up, nothing in her hair, no bra under her Indian-cotton blouse. An elephant-hair bracelet matched the black corduroy jeans and the buckled black slippers.

He put on his watch. 'Five-forty-five. Relax.'

'Promptness is the politeness of princes,' Vuissane quoted, adding 'and the duty of royal preceptors.' Behind the sardonic, roguish smile, he could see that she was excited to be the President's temporary 'preceptor'.

He scoffed, looking away: '*Bourgeoise.*'

She walked slowly to the bed and put her arms on his shoulders. It reminded him of a while before. As she leaned over to kiss him chastely, he felt the nipples, through the cotton, brush his own.

'Maybe I shall wait up for you tonight, if I am not exhausted.' She stood up. 'I feel more tense than before a show. I'm going to walk to the White House.'

'In this weather?' She was on her way out. 'Do you think the President likes the odor of female perspiration?' he asked.

'If the animal is young enough, probably.'

'Just pull the door after you.'

'*D'accord.*'

Before she closed the apartment door herself, he heard her throw in the Baltimore *Evening Sun* that was lying outside. He waited a few minutes before leaving the room to pick it up. Then, he walked to the kitchen to pour a Campari with plenty of ice and soda before he read the heading: 'Leak on Alaska Pipeline'. It must have been a quiet day in the world, he thought. The second story was on Camp David: It led with President Roberts' return to the White House in Marine One to prepare for his trip to Paris. Liversedge remained at what the *Sun* called the 'Catoctin retreat' as host to the prime minister of Israel and the first president of Palestine. The report from Thurmont was upbeat, but seemed to add nothing significant from the reporting of the day before. On page seven, he noticed that there had been a garbage-collectors' strike in Calcutta.

Back at his own apartment, Muir made the notes for the evening show. The music was pre-selected since a week before. He put off work on the book for another day.

He watched the network news at seven. There was nothing memorable there, either. He went back to his notes, adding a satirical thought, making a change of words that would cue him to tell an anecdote in a simpler, more direct way. He ate a light, cold dinner on the terrace, seeing the sun become a red halo behind Rosslyn. He went inside and watched the end of a public-television documentary on Iraq. Shortly after nine, he went down to the garage and began the drive out toward the radio station, near the District line, off upper Connecticut Avenue.

3

The commercial which had followed Mike O'Mara's program was over and the red light came on. He put the cough box down and said: 'Good evening. This is Donald Muir on the Evening Beat. It's been a beautiful day, and now darkness is upon us. Time to rap a little, listen to some music.' He paused, switching from the wistful to the sardonic.

'I guess you've all noticed that the news of the day is that there's been a strike by the garbage collectors in Calcutta. It's not an easy job, being a garbage collector in Calcutta, and I'm sure they've got a case. The mayor of Calcutta told me once 'No matter what you do, parts of this city will always be a slum.' I said: 'If Calcutta was in America, those parts wouldn't be a slum any more, your honor: They'd be an inner city'.'

He paused again, to allow people driving home along the Beltway to switch their minds from sales accounts to satire. He said: 'Have you ever thought how much we've become dependent on euphemisms? They help us tolerate the intolerable. They flatter those to whom we can't offer much else but our hypocrisies. Have you noticed that there's no class in America below the middle, and that small eggs are called 'medium'? Maybe Calcutta could have avoided giving their garbage collectors more pay if they'd copied us and called them the sanitation department.

'We call typists secretaries, and janitors maintenance engineers. Because homo-sexuals live lives of anxiety we call them gay. There was a time when we called self-indulgence doing your own thing — that's much better, right?'

He rambled on, without a pause. 'People don't suffer from starvation any more, only malnutrition. An underdevel-oped country is called a developing one, which is rather like a surgeon in an operating theater calling out 'Bring in the convalescent!' Some of our Third-World experts sing the praises of 'single-party democracy', which is roughly the same as talking about an atheist religion.'

He drew a breath, as a prelude to drawing a conclusion. 'Maybe we should just invent *more* euphemisms, on the theory that nothing succumbs like excess. Let's produce so many euphemisms that society terminates them with extreme prejudice. How about 'The number of people between jobs hit nine per cent'?

'Now Kojak's back, I'm waiting for him to tell some hoodlum: 'This time, baby, we've got you for involuntary euthanasia with a sports weapon, unilateral transfer of bank property, and sending fiction through the mails. You're looking at twenty years in a correctional facility'. And can't you hear the hoodlum replying: 'Pass away, you puppy'.'

He paused. Had he gotten Telly Savalas' accent right? He should have practised it, in the car.

'Well, enough of philosophy. Do any of you remember Django Reinhardt, the French gypsy who used to play jazz on the violin? Here he is with 'When the Saints . . . ' '

He put the needle on the desired spot, span the record a little to meet the motor's speed, and sat back. For two hours, he would be too busy, too tense to think of anything but the need to keep the program rolling, and to make it sound relaxed.

★　★　★

He glanced at the clock on the wall, the huge needle-like hand whacking out the seconds. Eleven-thirty. He sipped milk. He had two more 'sequences' left on his guideline notes, four numbers, some commercials, one of them to be read with extemporization. He had more time left than he needed. He would have to extend the next sequence. At this time of night, some other broadcasters who did this type of show would just gab on, stream-of-consciousness style. He had usually resisted that. But he would have to expand.

Roberta Flack wailed until the last ounce of carbon dioxide in her chest had been shared with the recording-studio technicians. He pushed the cassette for the termite-killer advertisement. When it was done, he said: 'I mentioned earlier the garbage-collectors' strike in Calcutta. Of course, the good news of today was a repeat of yesterday's good news.

'President Roberts, as you know, returned to Washington to prepare for his trip to France; but at Camp David, Vice President Roger Liversedge continues to play host to Palestine's first President and Israel's prime minister. There seem to have been no major problems at this first encounter between the newly-elected President abu Riad and prime minister ben Tewfiq, who is Israel's first Sephardic-Jewish head of government, the son of an immigrant Moroccan waiter.'

He paused. 'Peace in the Middle East is all well and good, but it poses a threat to a cherished institution. With this development, friends, whom are we going to be prejudiced against? We are supposed to be the most self-confident people on earth, but we seem to be lost without our prejudices — even without our prejudices against our prejudices.'

The comfortable thing about radio was that you always felt there was a good audience reaction, whether it was there or not. You had no showbiz tricks except your voice, and you knew that if your voice wasn't right they wouldn't let you do the program. He silently cleared his throat.

'You may recall, a month or so ago, I said I had hired a new woman to clean my apartment. I said she was black and I recounted a joke she told. You remember? I asked her where she came from and she said 'Pittsburgh. My parents were in the iron and steel industry.' And I said 'What?' And she said 'Yeah. She ironed and he stole'. Do you know? — I got nearly fifty letters of complaint for telling her story, all but a couple of them from white liberals, and I'll probably get some more.'

He was entering a thicket, but that was one of the things he was paid to do. He reminded himself of the number of thickets Gary Trudeau and Russ Baker had entered over the years. They were the commandos and he was only in a service corps. He went on: 'Time was when we could be prejudiced against a lot of people. Even if we belonged to one of the groups, we could still make fun of all the others. We could stick it to the darkies, the redskins, the yidds, the spicks, the shanty-Irish, the faggots, you name it.

'Have you heard the one about the Mexican who asked the Irishman if there was any equivalent of the word *mañana* in his language? And the Irishman said 'Well, therrre are siveral, but none that convey the same sense of urgency'.'

He paused, like a patter comedian giving time for canned laughter. He said: 'Well, all of that was taken away. Not only were we no longer allowed to make Polish jokes or associate the Wops with the Mafia, but we couldn't even have the privilege of believing that we were liberal because we didn't; we were taught to respect the blacks and the Indians at school, just as we were taught to respect the flag.

'So we hunted around and we found a loophole. No-one had said anything about socking it to the Arabs. It was a new form of anti-Semitism, to give it a fancy name, and since the Jews approved it was even a way of not being anti-Jewish. And we could invent reasons. They had oil, which was annoying, and some of them had money, which was downright disgraceful. Some of the Arab countries had a higher per capita income than the United States, which was impertinent, if not blasphemy.'

He looked at the clock. He had nearly filled the three minutes he had budgeted. It was time to stop rambling and put in the sting-in-the-tail.

'It isn't all over, but I think the welcome President abu Riad has received in this country says something. What it says is that, sometime soon, we're going to hear a lot of jokes about Ascension Islanders, and the Laplanders have got it coming. Never give up on Western civilization.

'And now, a strange symphony out of India, with Doti Singh on the zither, and . . . '

There would, he knew, be letters on that, perhaps phone calls. The most likely, he thought, would be a more-in-sorrow-than-anger complaint from a Cherokee in Silver Spring who would want to know why he had revived the term 'redskin'.

He walked over to the UPI ticker, and froze.

'BULLETIN,' it said. 'PRESIDENT ROBERTS DEAD.'

★   ★   ★

He read it twice. Underneath, it said: 'BULLETIN — PRESIDENT ROBERTS DIED TONIGHT IN THE WHITE HOUSE, THE VICTIM OF AN APPARENT HEART ATTACK.' For once, he regretted that the ticker in the studio had no bulletin bell.

The follow-up was saying that death had taken place about twelve minutes before, that it had been in his sleep, that he was sixty-two. Muir sat down at the console and faded out Doti Singh. He said: 'Friends, listeners, a very important, a very sad announcement. President Roberts died a few minutes ago in his sleep, the victim of an apparent heart attack. I repeat, President Roberts . . . '

His voice sounded mechanical. There were not too many different ways to make such an announcement, and nothing original would have sounded proper.

'President Roberts was sixty-two,' he was saying now. 'He was our fortieth president. Before being elected in 1980, he had served for three terms as a senator from Indiana. Before that, he was a congressman from an agricultural district in the state. Prior to entering politics, President Roberts had been a trial lawyer. His wife Ellen is currently in Australia on a semi-official visit.'

While he spoke, he awkwardly carried the microphone around the studio, searching for a suitable disk. He had decided against the national anthem, resting in its accustomed slot, because he did not want people who might be just tuning in to think that the night's broadcasting was over, and either switch off or switch to another wavelength. He found *America the Beautiful*. After the sentence about Mrs. Roberts' visit to Australia, he put it on. Then, he headed back to the ticker.

A message nearing completion said that the president had retired to bed at about eleven o'clock. It corrected the earlier dispatch saying that he had died in his sleep by saying that he had had time to ring a bell for his butler, Wong Hwan, who had hurried down from his quarters in a bathrobe 'to find the chief executive already deceased'. No kiss of life? Had Wong felt inhibited from blowing air down the head-of-stately throat? Maybe the Chinese didn't believe in reviving the dead. Wong had apparently called the duty physician, and the President's own doctor, Rear Admiral Morro, was on his way in from his house in Potomac, Maryland. The first 'take' of what would obviously be a very long biography started, beginning with Roberts' birth in Indianapolis in 1921.

America the Beautiful was almost over. When it finished, Muir said: 'For those of you who did not hear the news a moment ago, President Roberts . . . ' The shock of the news was almost over for him now. He would have to say something about the now-canceled trip to Paris. He thought of Vuissane. Would Liversedge go to Paris in Roberts' stead? Almost certainly, not at once. Now Muir's first personal reaction when he had read the news was bubbling to be expressed. He gave vent.

'President Roberts' death automatically brings to the Oval Office the first black president in United States history, Roger Vishnu Liversedge.' His Unitarian minister-father's choice of a Hindu deity for the second name had always seemed slightly absurd; now, it became a part of American history, and acceptable.

'Vice President Liversedge is currently at Camp David, which President Roberts left earlier today. Liversedge stayed on to play host to Abba ben Tewfiq, the prime minister of Israel, and President Ali abu Riad, the first head of the new Palestinian state. There's no news just yet of when Roger Liversedge will take the oath. I repeat, for those of you who've just tuned in, President Roberts . . . '

There would be a lot of people, getting the news from phone calls, who would be joining his audience. Muir was carrying the mike again, as he spoke, fingering through the station's tiny classical collection. He knew few of the pieces by name, what they sounded like. For safety, he chose Beethoven's Fifth Symphony. Drama.

While the symphony played, he crouched over the ticker again. More of Roberts' biography was flowing on. There was another news message, with more facts; then, more biography. Muir walked into a control booth, empty at night, and called Camp David. The Marine on the switchboard said Len Duval, Liversedge's press secretary, was on another line, with 'over forty calls' backed up.

'When's the new President being sworn?'

'I don't know, sir, but the judge is on her way right now from Emmitsburg.'

Muir faded Beethoven out at what sounded like a suitable point and reannounced the evening's news. He added that a judge was 'reportedly' on her way from Emmitsburg to administer the presidential oath. He mentioned the Paris trip that Roberts would not now fulfill.

'We've no other news from Camp David, but President abu Riad and premier ben Tewfiq have probably been informed of President Roberts' death. UPI says House Speaker Anthony Gentiluomo and other leading political figures are in the process of being informed and that messages are being sent by the State Department to embassies across the world.' He repeated the news again with suitable solemnity, ending with 'Roger Vishnu Liversedge will be the nation's forty-first president and the first black American to hold the high office.'

He faded Beethoven in again. There was no point in playing commercials about pantyhose and Rosenthal Chevrolet or reading the one about the new Turkish restaurant in Arlington. Through one ear of a headset, he let Beethoven flow over him, and for the first time in months he felt optimistic — and guilty about his reaction. Turning away from the dead microphone, as though someone in the outside world might actually hear him, he smacked his right fist into his left palm.

'Dammit, Don!' he said to himself out loud. 'You'll have a bestseller after all!'

★   ★   ★

A few seconds before twelve, he was glad to announce that 'in a moment, it will be Friday June 21. And now, no commercials tonight. I'm handing you over to your late, late-night host, Art Foster.' He continued to talk past the mike, looking only out of the corner of his eye at Foster, who was standing beside him, seeming dazed. 'Art, I know tonight's news has been a shock to everyone.'

'It sure has,' said Foster glibly. Normally, he would have taken over Muir's chair during the commercial. Now, Muir was wiggling out of it while trying not to move the chair, and Foster was doing a sidewise wiggle to take his place. 'A really dreadful shock,' Foster was saying. Muir knew he was wondering how he would get through three hours of what was normally pop and rock. 'Well, good morning, folks,' Foster was saying now, still reversing into a more comfortable position in the chair. 'It's Friday June 21, a few moments after midnight, and as you know, we shall shortly have a new president. A time for grief, a time for hope for the future of our country. Life goes on. I'll keep you informed of the breaking news from time to time. Now, Buddy King and the Night Crawlers with . . . '

Muir slipped out, closing the padded door, grinning.

* * *

Back at the Watergate, there was a message for him to call Carl, his editor at New Manhattan Library. The message listed Carl's home number. In the apartment, he poured himself a Campari and soda and reached for the phone; as his hand touched it, it rang. It was Carl.

'Hi, Don, figured you'd just be back from the studio. How do you feel?'

He heard himself saying, blandly: 'It was quite a surprise.'

Carl sounded more happy than surprised. 'How quickly can you finish? This is sure to mean a much bigger promotion budget, but the sooner you can complete, the better.'

'I'll have to incorporate some events of the next few weeks.'

' — that later,' Carl was saying. 'Can you finish in a week? You said the other day the draft was nearly there.'

'It still needs working. And I'll have to change a few points to allow for pre-knowledge by the reader that he's now President. The final chap — '

'Send us everything but the final chapter in a week. Can you do that?'

'Realistically, there's a lot of work to be done on the rest. Three weeks?'

' — what I'm there for. Trust me. Two weeks max, but ten days would be better. If I could have it special-delivery a week from Monday.'

'Okay.'

In the background, he could hear Carl's radio, but Carl repeated what he had heard. 'Liversedge has taken the oath. Did you hear that? He's leaving for the

White House shortly.'

When Carl hung up, Muir called Mike O'Donnell. His agent was asleep and spent about thirty seconds getting to the receiver. His voice sounded thick, as though he had quaffed too long at a Village pub. Perhaps it was just a sedative.

'What!' he exclaimed. He sounded mortified to know that the President had died. Then: 'Holy shit! We've got a bestseller! How did Roberts die? Oh, yeah. How soon can you finish? This must really give you some inspiration.'

Muir was reminded of someone saying to him one day, on the other side of the continent: 'You could put all the sincerity of Hollywood into the navel of a flea, and still have space left over for an agent's heart.' That was unfair, he thought; Mike was not a Hollywood agent.

'Yes,' he said, 'I just thought you'd like to know. Go back to sleep. I'll call you tomorrow.'

Vuissane must have gone to sleep, also; otherwise she would be there, or she would have called. Muir was half-glad. He was thinking about the book, something he had been trying to push to the back of his consciousness all week. It would have been nice to have a few drinks and to make love again; but, on second thoughts, anything like a celebration would have seemed misplaced to Vuissane, who had been with the President a few hours earlier, coaching his French. She would probably be upset. Apart from the household staff, she might have been the last person to see him alive.

He went to the terrace, cradling his drink and looking up the moonlit river. New ideas about improving the Liversedge biography suddenly seemed meaningful. He went back inside, fixed a second drink, returned to the terrace, sat back on the lounger and looked at the clear night sky. He had begun the book with the bombing raid in Korea, some snatches from the comments about Liversedge from other officers who had been with him then — the whole anecdote was recounted in more detail in Chapter Four. Now, perhaps, he should begin with the Inaugural.

* * *

It was nearly a half-hour later when two specks of light appeared at low altitude, somewhere near Great Falls. The double baritone buzz grew louder. The first helicopter, then the second, switched on landing lights, illuminating debris in the river. In about a minute, Roger Liversedge would be landing on the south lawn of the White House, the cameras recording the scene; old reporters who came to the White House only rarely now would be standing with the regulars, discussing past such occasions with each other; things like Johnson coming back from Dallas, twenty years before. Even taking the White House post seemed more attractive to Muir now, with Liversedge in the presidency. He decided he would do it for a year or so, until Roger retired from office. But he had already decided against going to the south lawn tonight. After Marine One passed, he would go inside and watch the arrival on television, and fix the image for his book.

The roar of Marine One on the humid night air was almost deafening. The presidential chopper was almost abeam of Thompson's Boatyard, barely a hundred yards away. Suddenly, there was a huge flash of fiery light and a deafening explosion. Marine One was a ball of fire. There was a massive splash as the heavy craft hit the water. Fire lingered on the surface for a moment. Then, there was darkness but for the landing and navigation lights of the secret-service chopper, hovering in the spot where Marine One had been, a moment before: One rotary blade from the destroyed aircraft emerged from the shallow water.

Muir felt dazed. The second helicopter was still lingering noisily and helplessly in the air: Inside, the rest of Liversedge's bodyguards would probably be shouting into the radio. Away to the right, through the trees, Muir's eye was attracted by a running figure, someone short; he or she was heading out of the boatyard parking lot, on to the sidewalk, and now off into the shadows under the overpass of the Whitehurst Freeway. Short hair, a masculine gait. Muir leaned from his parapet and looked sideways and down, then up at other balconies. Despite the explosion, they all seemed empty. After all, he reflected, it was past one A.M. People must be watching from their windows, where only the river would be in view. Had he alone seen the fleeing man? Should he have rushed down the corridor, waited for an elevator, gone downstairs and tried to follow?

Police sirens sounded, first one, then two, then a cacophony of banshees. The first cruiser arrived, coming down the Rock Creek Parkway; it turned right with a screech of tires and went through the parking lot at nearly forty miles an hour, then sped on across the grass with its kerb-climber tires, crushing a bush; its headlights illuminated the water underneath where Marine Two was hovering. The single rotary blade of Marine One remained as motionless as a tombstone. The other chopper was now about six feet above the water. What if Marine One had had pontoons? Might someone have survived? More police cruisers arrived, including one from the Park Police. The river was soon bathed in their headlights, while their spotlights probed in all directions. A civilian had appeared from somewhere; he was standing in the parking lot, talking to a police officer, pointing to the overpass, obviously describing the fleeing man, the direction in which he had gone. One cruiser took off, tardily, in pursuit.

Muir sat down on the lounger again, remembering the drink in his hand. He drank it down. What he had just seen still seemed unbelievable, yet he had been one of a very few people — the pilots of the support chopper, the man who was out there talking to the police — who had actually seen Roger die in a ball of flame, in front of their eyes. Speaker Tony Gentiluomo was now presumably waiting on the White House lawn to greet Liversedge; instead, he was about to learn that it was he, Gentiluomo, who was President.

Muir could not take his eyes from the stark theater of the river — the single blade, illuminated by helicopter and cruiser lights, grimly emerging from the water. Within about two hours, his book about the first black Vice President had become the book about the first black President and now also the book about the first president since Kennedy to be assassinated. But who had destroyed Marine One, and how — and why? They would probably know how by morning, but answering who and why might take longer. Any one of a number of people might have wanted to kill a black president.

He was surprised that none of the police had looked up at his lighted apartment and seen him there. There had been no 'Hey mister, did you see anything?' For all the police had known initially, the plane could have been fired on from the Watergate building itself. But if he went down now, he would really have nothing more to add. The pilots of Marine Two and the witness in the parking lot had seen everything there was to see. If he added his own corroboration, it might cost him several hours at the police station, at the FBI, with the Secret Service.

He tiptoed inside, grateful for the D.C. Police's inefficiency, and knocked off the switches. He went straight to bed, but it was to be a long time before he slept.

★   ★   ★

From the moment that he had witnessed the assassination, Muir's shock had been tempered by the guiltily pleasant feeling of surprise. Roger had been a friend, and a friend of long standing, but he had also become, for over eight months, a mountain of raw material. Over that period, Muir had begun to look at Roger's life as Roger's physician must have regarded Roger's body — as a subject separate from the persona. Roberts' death and Liversedge's inheritance of the presidency had been a definite plus for the book, and now the assassination made it perhaps the hottest literary property of the year. To grieve a death and to stand to profit from it was a sufficient dilemma in itself, but in this case it was magnified; in the first exuberance of reason that precedes sleep, Muir began wondering whether Roger's death had saved Roger's *Life*. At least, he thought, it had restored it.

Then as his brain relaxed further in the dark, and the biographer became once more the vicarious autobiographer, he began to think of Roger again only as a lifelong friend. It was a characteristic of Muir's that whenever he looked for long at some wellknown figure, he would fantasize on how that person must have looked in childhood. It was an exercise that he was most tempted to do with major criminals; but politicians, being equally controversial, also fitted into the game easily. At various times, he had found himself doing it with Leonid Brezhnev and Fidel Castro and various prime ministers of South Africa. In a museum, he had done it once with Tamerlane. Now, in Muir's mind, he saw Roger indulging in a humane discussion of world affairs, a week or so before, at Admiral's House, his official residence, and through the image came Roger in high-school baseball uniform. Muir had stressed in the book the atmosphere of rectitude combined with individual freedom in which Roger had grown up in his parents' house; but now that Roger had been murdered, Muir began to give his own words on that subject a meaning they had begun to lose from frequent rereading On the one hand, Muir thought, no-one in politics is pure, and the most successful least of all — and Roger had been successful, by any normal American yardstick. On the other, Roger had been special: more honest, both politically and otherwise, than most; a good soldier for the party, with all the compromises that that entailed, but a more decent human being than most of the others in the trade; a patrician, but not a snob; a professional prosecutor for most of his life, but never a vengeful or vindictive man.

He wondered how Roger would have felt if he, Muir, had died, and the death had somehow helped Roger politically. Then, as Muir's mind finally hazed into consciouslessness and the thoughts became harder to concentrate in linear progression, he was aware only that he had lost a friend. But the subconscious knowledge that he had also gained an investment from that loss still leavened the feeling of depression. He slept soundly.

Part Two

The Days That Followed The Night That Everyone Remembers

1

In his dream, he was in a judge's chambers with Carl and Mike and Steve Morton and some attorneys. The judge was fat and jovial. Everyone seemed relaxed except Muir and a small man of about sixty who looked furtively and distrustfully at everyone else. The little man looked like Central Casting's idea of a minor mobster. He looked like the person whom Muir had imagined in his mind when he had written of the accusation that Liversedge had allowed a Mafia case to be fixed. With the mobster was a tall, glib-looking attorney about half his age who was whispering confidently and rather unctuously to the little man; the little man was whispering back audibly: 'I didn't kill no president.' The judge was deciding where everyone should sit. Muir felt uncomfortable. He knew that the killing of a president had been helpful to him. He held back from the table, but the judge said: 'Don, come and sit next to me. You'll enjoy this cucumber soup.' Muir noticed then that the conference table had place settings and that in front of the chair offered to him was a steaming tureen of white and green liquid. It looked appetizing. There were bowls in place. He sat down and helped himself. A phone rang, and the judge shouted to a young woman clerk who metamorphosed into Muir's vision: 'Tell whomever it is to call back, we're having lunch.' But the phone went on ringing, and Muir woke up, recollected the night before, and shook himself out of bed at once.

'Hello.'

'Donald Muir?'

'Yes.' He wondered what time it was. Judging by the sun on the river, it was already nine o'clock.

'Listen carefully. I'm in the Howard Johnson's across the street from you. We want to tell you why we offed that supercilious black bastard. You're writing a book, aren't you? You mentioned it on your show once.'

'Yes. I can't speak now. There's someone with me,' Muir lied. 'Give me a number to call.' Was he reacting correctly, he wondered; he still wasn't quite awake.

'No can do, feller.' The caller had a modified southern accent, a typical Washington tone. 'Just clear the decks. Someone will call you in fifteen or twenty minutes about a date.'

'Fine.'

Muir stabbed at the receiver rest and called his usual source at the FBI.

'Mr. Raines is busy,' said a woman's voice.

'It's very, very urgent. It's absolutely, absolutely urgent. I've got to speak to him now.'

'He's on long-distance,' the middle-aged voice crabbed. He sensed that she was lying.

'It's urgent, urgent! Get him off!'

'I can't — '

'Get him off, you moron, or I'll have you fired.'

'Sir, he's talking to the deputy director — '

'Tell him it's urgent, don't you understand? The assassination.'

'Just a moment, sir. What was your name?'

If he said 'Muir', Jack Raines would think he was calling as a reporter, and might merely offer to call him back. He said: 'Just say Max. He'll understand.' Raines wouldn't, of course, understand: There was no reason why he should. But he had told her that it concerned the assassination.

'Raines.'

'Jack? Don. Don Muir. I've had a call from someone who claims he did it.'

'The assassination?'

'Yep. Tap my line and trace. Someone is supposed to be calling back in fifteen minutes, about a date. I don't know whether it will be the same person, but I suspect not. A woman perhaps, since he said a date.'

'Why'd he call you? Sounds like a crazy.'

'Could well be. Can you tap this number quickly?'

Muir was struck with the absurdity of

the conversation — a journalist asking the FBI to tap his line.

'Give it to me again.'

When Muir put down the receiver, he went to the bedroom and collected the espresso machine. He was putting in fresh coffee when the phone rang again. It was Vuissane.

'Oh Donald, it's dreadful.'

'I saw it,' he said. 'From the terrace.'

'That too. He was your friend. I meant the President, Mr. Roberts.'

Of course. 'Yes, you were with him, only a few hours before.'

'He seemed fine.' She sniffed, as though she might be crying. 'Come down. I have to speak to you. *Mon per* — '

'Wait. We'll talk of that when I come down, not on the phone.'

He knew she was about to talk of her labor permit, the one she didn't have. It was an almost daily recurrence in their conversations, but Muir felt exasperated that she should be concerned about it now, even though she had said something the night before about getting President

73

Roberts to pull some strings. A year before, by prolonging a singing visit, Vuissane had joined the five-figure horde of illegal aliens in Washington; but Muir didn't want her discussing this when the FBI might already be tapping his line.

'Come now,' she said. 'I'm shaken.' *Ebranlée*. It sounded rather like a formal diagnosis.

'I'll come right away.'

He forgot about coffee. He had to be back in ten minutes to get the 'dating' call. In his pajamas, he hurried into the corridor and down the firestairs to Vuissane's floor. He found her door open. Vuissane was sitting on the side of her bed, her face hidden by hair and hands. He sat down beside her; she buried her face in his shoulder.

'I can't believe he could die like that. And Mr. Liversedge, too.'

She didn't seem to have focused clearly on Roger's assassination; she was principally distraught about Roberts, her language student of the evening.

'We all knew he had a heart condition,' Muir said.

'But just like that!' She held out her hands, as though gesturing toward a corpse. Then her face was once again hidden, like a nursing kitten's, in his shoulder.

'I'm expecting a very important call,' he said softly. 'What's this about your permit?'

'He said he would arrange it. The President . . . And now . . . '

Her concern for Roberts and her concern for herself seemed incongruous. He said: 'Perhaps Mrs. Roberts will help you. Not right away, of course. Besides, your lawyer said — '

'He was such a kind gentleman.' She was obviously talking of Roberts again. Resting his cheek on the silky dome of her head, Muir half-smiled sardonically. A *gentil monsieur*. It was a better epitaph than the old pol deserved, one he would be happy with, Muir thought — then he felt guilty about applying the same cynicism to Roberts in death that he had applied to him in life.

'Try not to worry. You have to sing tonight at Rufus'.'

'You must be, what can I say — about Mr. Liversedge. Does it affect your book?'

'It enhances it.'

'Of course.' She seemed bewildered.

'You're naturally shocked about President Roberts' death,' Muir said. 'You were with him such a short time before; it must be terrible. I didn't realize that your principal reason for cultivating the White House was to get your labor permit solved. I'm sure your lawyer will work it out.'

'That creep,' she said. Now there were real tears, but they seemed to be tears of anger. 'The President would have done it like that, as a favor.' Vuissane resented the legal process, resented lawyers. The one she had, had neither an office, a secretary or a library, and worked out of his small apartment, but by charging forty dollars an hour he made more than bigger attorneys demanding two and a half times as much.

'I wish I'd been a lawyer,' she said.

He wanted to tell her she was being distracted and irrational. Instead, he said: 'Your voice would have been wasted in court. The judge would be saying 'Eh? What's that? I can't understand your accent, counsel'.'

'You don't take me seriously.'

'Vuissane, a friend, the new President of the United States, has just been — murdered. And so far as I know, no-one yet knows why. If I took life seriously, I'd cry every day.'

'I'm glad you don't.' The exchange — the nearest they had ever come to a quarrel — had relaxed her.

'I have to decamp,' he said.

'Go. I'm all right now.'

She had called to him as though to a father, not just because of the shock of Roberts' death, but for her own sake — the permit problem. It was almost comic — as though Roberts' death was not a national affair, but a family inconvenience. In Muir's experience, everyone always seemed to get their permits, sooner or later; there never seemed to have been a time, since he returned from overseas, when he didn't know about half a dozen talented foreigners, all seeking labor permits. But

Vuissane lived in fear of being arrested, expelled, and embarrassed. There had been that partly irrational fear in her voice when she spoke of Roberts' death. She could never have too much reassurance. Her parents had been separated when she was very young, and Muir knew that he had to play two roles — lover and father. Now he felt warm about Vuissane's cockeyed reaction. Roberts, the kind uncle, had died before giving her the gift which he had promised, and so she both mourned and resented his death, crying for Roberts and for herself.

★   ★   ★

Muir found he had left his apartment door open. From well down the corridor, he could hear the phone. He grabbed at the receiver, dropped it, picked it up again.

'Don Muir.'

'My name's Frank Abrams. Rabbi Frank Abrams. I heard you last night, with your twisted logic about prejudice. Let me tell you something, smart-ass. Six million Palestinians didn't die in the Holocaust.'

He put the receiver down and went back to the coffee machine in the kitchen. Two American presidents had died, and there were people still thinking about his broadcast? Muir recalled his first-ever editor saying: A journalist should never, ever, be surprised. There were probably people in Washington who were worried that the assassination had spoiled their lifetime visit to the capital.

The phone rang again. Was it the loonie? In the trade, all emotional protest callers were classified as loonies. He couldn't take the risk of missing the man who said he was the killer, or part of a conspiracy.

'Yes?'

'Don't you hang up on me. I have a right to be heard.'

'I'm waiting for an important call,' Muir said softly. 'I need the line clear.'

'Oh, sure,' said the caller, sarcastically.

Muir said: 'Eagle One, this is Fishtrap Nine. Trace this individual and bring him in. He sounds like a diversion.'

'Hey, what is this?'

'I repeat: Eagle One, this is Fishtrap Nine. Do you have this call? Hold him for questioning. Over and out.'

He heard the click of the caller's phone. The ruse had apparently worked. He recalled another of his first editor's maxims: Never overestimate the enemy, they're as dumb as they look.

The next five minutes were long. He collected the morning papers, which he had left lying at the door when he had rushed in to take Abrams' call. The expected call from Howard Johnson's, or wherever, was overdue. Had the loonie blocked the line at the wrong moment?

He read the *Post*, but it was clear from the first two paragraphs of the main analysis story that nobody had anything but hypotheses. While reading, he was listening to one of the all-news radio stations. There too, the assassination story seemed wrapped in confusion. Suddenly, he remembered that he badly needed his morning coffee, and it was then that the phone rang again.

A young woman's voice, even more

southern than that of the man who had called earlier, ostensibly from Howard Johnson's, said: 'Donny boy, if you're not too busy with all that's happening in our fair capital, how's about lunch at Jean Louis' place?' The sexiness of her tone seemed exaggerated. This, he concluded, was the 'date'.

'Twelve be okay?' he said.

'Noon is fine.'

Jean-Louis' place . . . That could only mean the Niçoise restaurant on Wisconsin, where a chef of that name did a comedy act in the late evening. Everyone in Georgetown knew the place, the act. Muir called Raines.

'Yes, we got it,' Raines said with satisfaction. 'How can they be so reckless? I think it's a game. Where do they mean?' Muir told him. 'We'll have someone there.'

'No-one too obvious, please.'

'Count on us. What was the Abrams fellow calling about? I thought your trick was a bit nervy.'

'I get calls like that every week. Usually I cover them with syrup.'

'I hope you always report any threats.'

'Let's talk about that some other time,' Muir said, conscious that he was becoming agitated himself.

★　★　★

Coffee was finally made. Mike O'Donnell called. Muir went on reading the papers while he spoke to him. Then, the doorbell rang. Muir ended the conversation with Mike, put down the phone, and opened up.

'Hwan!'

Wong Hwan, President Roberts' butler, looked crestfallen, his thin face haggard under an old-fashioned fedora.

Muir had not been expecting callers, and certainly not Wong Hwan. He had known the quiet Taiwanese with the Hollywood-Chinese accent since Wong had worked for Liversedge in Providence. He had become a familiar face who brought them drinks while Liversedge talked, and once or twice Hwan had been drawn into the conversation. Muir had seen him only rarely, at Liversedge's, since he moved to the White House job.

'You've lost two good friends,' Muir said, edging Wong toward a sofa.

'Plezident die in my arms,' Wong said. 'Wannedoo talk to someone.'

'Of course you did. I understand. Did you try to revive Mr. Roberts?'

'Never tink of it till too late. Too — too — '

'I understand. Coffee?'

'Oh. Prease.' He paused, as though weighing a question. 'Gov'nor Riv'sedge. Jus' ow' tair? You see it.'

'Yes.' Muir remembered how, even after Roger became Vice President, Wong had retained the habit of calling him 'Governor'.

'Tell me. Prease.'

Muir fetched a cup and poured coffee, recounting what he had seen, but leaving out the information about the fleeing figure, which was not in the *Post* or on the radio news. There must, he felt, be the obvious reason for that — the police didn't want the assassin forewarned.

When he had finished, Wong seemed more composed. To relax him further,

Muir said: 'Hwan, where were you born? Taipei? I don't think you ever told me.'

'Taiwan.'

'I know, but where?'

'Not Taipei. Small village.'

Muir was thinking that he should say a little more about Wong Hwan in the book. He was, after all, a feature of Roger's orientophilia, which he had acquired in Korea.

'You were brought to the United States by a general, Governor Liversedge used to say.'

'Gen'lal Schwarzmuller.' It seemed the only difficult name he had learned to pronounce correctly. 'He kin' man. I work for him as houseboy in 'Forty-five. Then he bling me here, sen' me to school, get me in Army.'

'You were a caterer.'

'Rater. First, I in artirrely.' He made a grotesque motion of firing some weapon. 'Cateler, rater. In Pentagon, for Gen'lal Forbes. From Lode Island. When I letire from Army, Gen'lal Forbes fin' me job with Gov'nor.'

When Liversedge had been elected Governor, Muir recalled, there had been speculation in the Providence *Journal* that, since he was the state's first black chief executive, he would be the first one in fifty years to have an all-white domestic staff. Liversedge had responded by saying that, although symbols were important, jobs were more so, and he was not firing anyone who did not want to leave. He had replaced the departing butler by Wong. Forbes, Muir guessed, must have had some inkling of Roger's taste for the orient, perhaps from some mutual acquaintance in Korea.

'President Roberts stole you away,' Muir said, smiling.

'It was jus' before — uh — '

'The party convention.'

'So. When Missa Loberts choose Missa Riv'sedge. He come to Gov'nor's mansion.'

Muir knew the story. It had been Roberts' first chance to have a long conversation with his future vice president, to size him up before he made his decision. Muir remembered Liversedge saying how Roberts had congratulated him on Wong.

'At end of evening,' Wong said, 'Missa Loberts say to me 'When I elected, as I gonna be, how you rike work for me at White House?' '

It was typical of Roberts, Muir had thought before, and thought again, that he had seen no rudeness in stealing Roger's butler in front of his eyes; after all, Roberts must have thought, he was going to make Liversedge Vice President; Liversedge would owe him plenty.

Wong was going on with his story. 'So I say, if Gov'nor Riv'sedge aglee. An' Gov'nor Riv'sedge, he say okay.'

Wong was looking toward the window, toward the terrace where Muir had watched the assassination.

'Awful. Awful. Who do such ting?'

Muir was touched that Wong Hwan had come to him, as a friend of Roger's whom he could talk to. Wong, from his period at Governor's Lodge, knew his employer and Muir had been friends since childhood. The butler was a lonely man, a widower, who carried his disculturation with him wherever he went. He had seemed to like working for Liversedge, and he must have been proud of his White House post. But he was not a man who easily showed his feelings, except occasionally about Taiwan. Muir remembered how he had refused to be interviewed for a profile in the New York *Times*. They had had to talk to others to get the story, the accounts of his special Chinese exercises, his jogging on the White House lawn. A very private man, proud of having served in the U.S. Army and the White House, and now, it seemed, proudly private in his sorrow about his last two employers.

'What will you do now?'

'Cannot tink. Too — too — '

'I understand.'

There was an awkward silence. Then, Wong said: 'You mus' be teb'bly busy, sir.'

'I'm afraid that's true.'

The phone rang.

'Won' keep you. No. Don' bodder come to door. May I call on you again?'

'Of course, any time. Come at the weekend. Things should be less hectic by then. Sunday?'

'Okay. I'll call firs', nes' time.'

Wong was on his way out. Muir said to the receiver: 'Yes? Donald Muir here.'

'Listen, I know you must have been fooling me just now. Hello?' The caller paused. 'Hello? This is Abrams. Last night's drivel — '

He put the receiver down again. Instead of irritating him, the comedy of the call, after Wong's visit, made him feel better; but at once he called the desk downstairs.

'Take all my calls for the next hour.'

★   ★   ★

He was reading *The Wall Street Journal* on the terrace — it was an early edition, with Roberts' death but not Liversedge's — when he heard a series of rings at the door, as though he had missed an earlier sound. Had Wong Hwan forgotten his hat? But Wong was surely too polite to ring a doorbell impatiently like that.

There were two men at the door, and they were unmistakable. They flashed simuli-leather cases with their FBI badges within.

'May we bother you?' said one of them.

'Come in.' In the living room, he pointed toward the sofa where Wong had been. Before sitting down, the man who had spoken at the door said: 'Collins. Fred Collins. This is Peter Cavalli.'

Muir nodded individually at each of them and they lowered themselves carefully, as though the sofa was made of glass. Collins was fortyish with a beer paunch and sandy hair. Cavalli was dark-haired and dark-eyed, about thirty, not quite so stocky. They both had short haircuts and wore off-the-hook double-knits, despite the summer heat outside.

'Beer?' asked Muir.

Collins shook his head. 'We're on duty.' Muir felt like saying: I never guessed. Instead, he said: 'I understood you were coming to the restaurant.' He thought: Is this what Jack Raines means by 'not too obvious'?

'The restaurant?' Collins looked inquiringly at Cavalli. Cavalli looked expressionlessly back, as though not believing something.

'Raines said — '

'Pardon? Raines? Jack Raines? Do you know him?'

'I was speaking to him a while ago.'

'We're from firearms and explosives. He's political.'

'Oh, you're not — uh — here on his instructions.'

'No. We work closely with the Bureau of Alcohol, Tobacco and Firearms. I didn't know you'd been contacted by Mr. Raines.'

Muir didn't bother to correct him, to say that it was he who had contacted Raines.

'It doesn't matter. Our work is different,' Collins went on. He looked at Cavalli for corroboration. Cavalli said 'Hmm', still expressionlessly; he had brought out a notebook. Collins said, politely: 'You don't mind if we take notes?'

Muir was tempted to say, pokerfaced, that he *did* mind, that he had a phobia about notebooks being opened in his home on Fridays. He checked the mischievous impulse quickly.

'Not at all.'

Collins reached for his own notebook.

'First of all, did you hear anything?'

Muir paused, understanding at last. So they had merely come to him as to anyone — no doubt, everyone — with balconies on the river.

'I not only heard it, I watched it.'

Even Cavalli stirred.

'Tell — I'm sorry,' he said, deferring to Collins.

'Yes, tell us what you saw.'

Muir told them.

'What color was the fire?' Collins asked.

'Orange. Yes, I guess you'd say orange.'

'Orange,' said Collins, as though he needed time to write the word down, and wanted Muir to pause again.

'How tall were the flames, from the nadir to the apogée?' asked Cavalli. This seemed to be his specialty.

'Excuse me?' Then he realized what Cavalli had said. 'Like a rocket explosion,' he said.

'A small missile?' asked Collins.

'Could have been, yes.'

'You in Nam?' Collins went on.

'Yes.'

'Might it have been a Strela?' He was naming a small Soviet missile.

'Might have been a Redeye or a Stinger,' said Muir, offering American equivalents. 'Or that Swedish thing — RBS — uh — '

'Interesting,' said Collins.

But their interest seemed to die from that point on. There were a few more questions, and then they left, having apparently got the confirmation which they had been seeking.

'We may be back,' Collins said.

'Any time,' said Muir.

★   ★   ★

He finished the papers, then called Len Duval and got Duval's harried female assistant. The bodies from Marine One had been recovered from the Potomac before dawn, he learned. The two presidents would lie in state in the Rotunda of the Capitol from the following evening.

President Gentiluomo had not yet moved into the Oval Office. Ellen Roberts would land at Andrews Air Force Base early the following day.

At ten minutes before twelve, he headed down to the garage. He would be a few minutes late, but if his 'date' was on time that would make it easier for her to spot him, as he came in.

He sat in the restaurant for an hour and a half and ate *rognons chablis*. No-one came to his table except the waiter. He spent part of the time writing on a napkin, expanding on an old recollection that had come to mind of a lunch in a Providence restaurant with Liversedge, and wondering between bites if he would ever meet Carl's new deadline for the book if he had to keep pursuing the assassination. Why had he taken that telephone call seriously?

At the coffee stage, a graceful, tall, patrician young woman of about Vuissane's age walked over and said: 'May I join you? We're mutual friends of Jack Raines'.'

Her waiter was following with her

coffee; he was on rollerskates, like most of the staff at the Niçoise. When he had gone, she said: 'Don't be disappointed. We suspected it might be a prank. But because she didn't come doesn't mean that it necessarily was. Maybe they got cold feet. Maybe anything. Maybe she came and just watched you, but I don't think so. Nobody seemed to be paying much attention to you. It was obvious who you were, even without Raines' description, because you were constantly watching the door, and you looked anxious every time a woman came in alone. Anyway, I'm sure you will keep in touch with Mr. Raines.'

She slipped him a twenty-dollar bill.

'I hope that will take care of your lunch,' she said coolly. 'The Bureau thanks you for your cooperation.' She gave a set smile, lifted her expensive-looking bag to her lap, rose to her full height and walked leisurely out, pausing at the door to congratulate the maître d'hôtel on the food.

* * *

Back home, he got out the manuscript. He was about to call the desk and ask the clerk there to take his calls when the telephone rang.

'Donald?' It was a woman's voice with a New England twang. He didn't recognize it at first. 'It's Adelaide. How are you?'

It was Roger's sister, the only close surviving relative, up in Newport.

'Shaken. How are you?'

'These things are sent to try us, Donald. Poor Roger, though.' She sounded composed, unanxious to burden others with her grief. 'How's the book?'

'Progressing.'

'It's very important, now. It will be Rolly's monument.' She was four years older, and her brother had been 'Rolly' in infancy.

'I certainly want to do my best.'

'I know you will, Donald.' She paused. 'Donald, I'm flying down to Washington this afternoon. I wonder if you could get me a hotel room, and of course I want very much to see you.'

'I'll get you into the Watergate hotel, next door.'

'That would be just fine.'

'What time do you arrive at the airport? I'll pick you up.'

'You must be terribly busy — '

'I'll pick you up.'

'So kind, Donald. I think it's — ' he imagined her slipping her glasses on — 'yes, five after five. Allegheny.'

★ ★ ★

She was tall and skinny. Like her father, she had never been good-looking, only distinctive. She was slightly darker than Roger, who had resembled her mother. As Muir saw her appear in the exit lane, he almost recognized her suitable black straw hat, which he had never seen before, better than the sharp, rather nondescript features. She was in black chiffon, black net gloves. Her single piece of expensive hand luggage bore a calligraphed 'A.C.L.' Like her brother, Adelaide Clytemnestra Liversedge had never married.

'Rather warm,' she said, as they emerged from the terminal. 'It's nice up in Newport just now.' The face was strained with grief, which showed on her thin features more than similar feelings would have shown on Roger's, but the tone was polite, friendly, unemotional. In the car, she said: 'Was he badly crushed?'

'I think he was.'

'Then I'll let them work their wiles on him before I go to see him.' She was obviously referring to the morticians.

He checked her in at the hotel.

'After you've freshened up, perhaps you'd like to come next door.' He gave her his apartment number.

'I'd like that, Donald.'

★ ★ ★

Adelaide sat on the terrace and commented on the view.

'Did Roger ever come here?'

'Only once. Wherever he went, he had to have his security people. He couldn't just drop in.'

'Of course not. And before that, he was pretty much always in Providence, wasn't he?'

'Virtually always.'

She sipped at her brandy, and went on: 'If he hadn't become Vice President, he would hardly have seen the world at all. I think it was during the campaign that he first saw America!' She gave a little laugh. 'I used to tell him that. I've been round the world three times. I've even been to Tibet.'

She was a school teacher, but she had always somehow managed to save enough money to travel.

'Yes, apart from Korea, he was a stay-at-home.'

'Still, I think he achieved everything he wanted to achieve, don't you? He never expected to be President, of course. And of course he barely was.'

It was the nearest she came to making a sort of appeal for pity. She went on: 'When I told you about our childhood, did I tell you about Uncle Rodney and Rolly's first bike?'

'Yes, you did.'

'We thought he would be an engineer, he was so good at repairing things, so precise in everything he did. Daddy wanted him to be a minister, but it was really only law he loved. He really did rather well at it, didn't he?'

'He surely did.'

She sipped at her brandy again, for composure. 'I was always a little surprised when he branched into politics.' She had told him that before, when he had questioned her, in Newport, specifically for the book; but he nodded to show interest. She went on: 'Of course, to be attorney general, you have to be political. I can't help regretting, now, that he didn't go into private practice, and the Bench.'

'He might have made the Supreme Court.'

'He might, Donald. That's just what I was thinking. He might well.'

She had finished her brandy. He picked up her glass and went inside to refill it. When he brought it back to the terrace, she was saying 'such a little rascal'. He had missed the start of the sentence, presumably something about childhood.

'He always had a fund of stories,' she said.

'He certainly loved to recount stories,' Muir agreed.

'Such naughty stories, sometimes,' Adelaide said.

'Yes, he certainly had quite a repertory.'

'I hope they're not all in the book.'

'Only a few that are relevant.'

'Of course. I trust your judgment.'

★   ★   ★

That evening, from the studio, he talked only about Liversedge, and he offered no humor that he expected anyone else to grasp. He wondered if Adelaide was listening. From time to time, he read items from the ticker, including the preparations going on in the Rotunda. He ran through several anecdotes that were in his book. He even mentioned the book itself — a shameless plug.

He told of Roger's arrival in the Middle East a year before, shortly after the full Israeli withdrawal from Gaza, the new furor over the West Bank settlements, and the breaking of relations by Cairo with Tel Aviv. Everyone knew that Liversedge had gone on from Egypt and Israel to some of the Gulf capitals and had immediately faced a threat of oil-price rises over the West Bank question. Now, wondering to himself if Carl would be irritated, Muir told the most momentous single revelation in the book.

This was that shortly after Liversedge had left Washington for Cairo, he had been briefed on the arrival, off Port Said, of a Libyan submarine bearing nuclear missiles in its torpedo shafts. The new government in Tripoli, entirely under Cairo's control, was prepared to make a surgical strike on Haifa and Tel Aviv if a timetable for a final Israeli withdrawal from the occupied territories was not agreed to. The president of Egypt had informed the local CIA station chief, with the diplomatic pretense that the initiative was Libyan and one which Egypt might not be able to countermand.

Liversedge had kept the nuclear component in the talks out of sight of the correspondents traveling with him. It was agreed in Cairo that he should inform Israel about the threat, but not the submarine's location — to preclude pre-emption. In return, he drew a graphic picture for the government in Cairo about the dangers of Israeli retaliation. Then he had gone on to Riyadh and Tehran, ostensibly to brief leaders there on the talks which he had held so far. In addition, he urged the petroleum capitals to replace the nuclear component in the dispute with a threat to triple the price of oil, since this would make it easier for Washington to pressure Israel on the occupation question.

Muir's listeners knew well, already, about the oil-price threat of the year before, but not about the submarine story. Muir explained that this had never been revealed by Washington, afterward, because it had later turned out to be an exquisite bluff; the submarine had been there, all right, but Libya, it was discovered later, still possessed no nuclear missiles. The misinformation about the submarine's ordnance had been believed because it could neither be confirmed nor denied — radiation in deep water cannot be detected from the air. The submarine itself had soon been picked up by U.S. spyplanes, but it had remained invulnerable: Its destruction, it was assumed at the time, would have led to irradiating the ocean and the atmosphere for miles around. Meanwhile, of course, as Muir's story from Liversedge now made clear, the Egyptian ploy had succeeded. Israel had agreed to a withdrawal; 'Peace in our decade' — Roberts' words — had come to the Middle East, and Liversedge and the oil states had received the credit.

'To a large degree,' Muir summarized, 'Liversedge *was* the catalyst. Here was a Machiavellian plan, concocted by a small-state lawyer who had served in Korea and who saw that any alternative to war would be preferable; but who knew that alternatives to war had to offer at least the same chances of success. Because of the risks of escalation, if nuclear weapons, unused since World War Two, were ever used again except for saber-rattling, Roger Liversedge thought he held the peace of the world in his hands that week. And, perhaps, after all, he did, since he defused the Middle East bomb itself.

'President Roberts, of course, had to approve his vice president's stratagem — agreeing that if it failed, whether oil prices actually rose, and by how much, would make little difference to a world faced by nuclear war.'

Muir cleared his throat silently, and concluded: 'Roger Liversedge joked to me a few weeks ago about how typically American his solution had been: To prevent two antagonists from fighting, he had suggested that a third party pretend to blackmail the United States and its allies, thus proving that money is more powerful than bombs. While you ponder on all this, here's the late Dean Martin singing 'My Way'.'

The ludicrousness of using the song as theme music for diplomatic history appealed to Muir, especially in the light of the false assumptions under which Roger had been working. It would, he guessed, have appealed to Roger.

Most of the music Muir played that evening was symphonic jazz of a subdued variety — small combos with double basses in place of drums, and one that featured a spinet instead of a grand piano. He had called the station earlier and asked Susie-Jo, who usually helped him with such chores, to look out a few nostalgic songs as well. That was how 'My Way' had turned up. He had spoken again about Roger's taste for the elegant restraint of oriental peoples. Because Roger had particularly liked a Japanese jazz singer, Muir had arranged, through Susie-Jo, to borrow a rare recording of her from Felix Grant at WMAL. He had found a suitable spot for that — an anecdote about the Tokyo trade talks — which he hoped would make it sound sardonic only to himself and Roger's ghost. He had started the evening with one of his own favorites, an Australian woman called Ginger Ford doing 'Solitaire'. This had set his theme about Liversedge — the private person projected into world events without losing his gift for privacy.

At eleven-thirty-five, while the Rosenthal Chevrolet ad was playing, he walked into an empty control room to see if anyone had left cigarettes. He hadn't smoked cigarettes for three years, and now suddenly three years' yearning occurred at once. The phone was ringing.

'WZYX. Can I help you?' he said.

'Donald Muir?' It was the southern-belle voice.

'Yes.'

'I've called you four times, during the commercials.'

'I can't hear the phone in the studio. I was just in this room by chance. What's doing?'

'I'm sorry I stood you up. I was there, but you were being watched. The fuzz, or the Hooverlets.'

'Really? Who was it?'

'A woman.'

Had the caller really been there, and left when she spotted the tall FBI agent? How had she known who the woman was? Or was she just making this up, and it happened to fit?

'I didn't notice.'

'I'll come tomorrow. Same time, same place. Please tell no-one.'

'I promise.' He meant it. Maybe it would be better without the FBI woman tailing him; perhaps she really was too obvious in her way, despite her thoroughly Georgetown look.

'I want to tell you everything, then give myself up.'

'*You* did it?' Had that been a woman, after all, whom he had seen running off under the freeway?

'Yes,' she said.

'Why are you doing this?'

'Giving myself up? Because I'm guilty.'

'No, why are you telling me?'

'I want to give you the story. It will be my parting gift. Won't it be a scoop?'

The layman's word usually made him shudder, but all he said was 'Sure.'

'For six months, your voice in the evening has been the only thing I live for. Do you hear what I'm saying, Donald?'

The world seemed full of loonies. He said: 'Why did you do it?'

107

'I'll tell you tomorrow. You should have guessed.'

'For the story? Just for the story?'

She avoided a direct answer. '*Your* story, Donald.' The voice was mellifluous. 'I have only one request. Before I turn myself in, I want you to come back with me. Just once.'

'You don't know me.'

'I listen to you every night. I've waited outside the studio and watched you go home. I knew if I approached you, you'd tell me to get lost. I know you must get other calls, other admirers. Donald, your voice.'

He was at a loss for words. Was she really a voice-fetishist? Well, his first attraction to Vuissane had been because of her voice. It was the only part of a person's brain you ever heard; you could tell a lot from a voice. If it wasn't for voices, blind people would surely never get married. The caller was saying: 'I promise you I'm pretty. I have a good body. I will love you so you'll remember me after they put me in the fryer.'

He ignored the unexpected, jarring

phrase on which she had ended.

'Your name?'

'No name. Miss No-Name. Tomorrow, Donald.'

'Who was the guy who called me first?'

'Him? My husband. Forget about him.'

'Crazy.'

'Perhaps, but I'll only bother you this once. And it will be *your* story.' He heard the click.

God! There was silence going out on his program! He rushed through the door and to the microphone and apologized for 'a slight technical hitch'. He announced the next number and set it going.

He went to the ticker. He was reading items aimlessly. There was something about a 'disturbance' in the Washington *Post* building. It wasn't clear what was meant from what he read. Something about a black demonstration. He couldn't concentrate. He went back to his console. He would not, of course, he decided now, go to the Niçoise again. The whole thing was absurd. The woman was demented, for sure. She could not possibly be coming at all.

At last, it was possible to say: 'In a moment, it will be midnight. Art Foster is in the studio, waiting to take over. For the next two nights, from ten to twelve, you'll be listening to Inge Wendahl with The Weekend Sound. Friends, listeners, goodnight. Have a pleasant weekend. And now, this message.'

He plugged in the Ford jingle and got up. Foster took his seat and said something to him. Muir was thinking about the telephone call he had just received and did not reply. He pulled the padded door to, softly, and walked through the corridor to the front of the building. Was she out there, watching his car? He drove home, occasionally watching in the driving mirrors. No-one seemed to be following.

Vuissane was waiting, in his bed. After they made love, she sobbed herself to sleep, and in her sleep she murmured about the *gentil monsieur*. Henry Roberts.

2

The middle-aged, male, black reception-ist in the hall of the Post stood up authoritatively: He looked anxious as the thirty-four black men and one big black woman, all wearing unseasonal top coats, milled in through the glass doors. A tall, thin, brownskinned man with an icy stare and a shaven head preceded the visitors to the desk.

'We want to publish an announce-ment.'

'Advertising's on the other side,' said the receptionist offhandedly.

The shavenheaded man swung round and faced the others.

'Bismillah, action!' he said.

Everyone produced M-16s.

'Bismillah, don't nobody move!' said the big woman.

The few people milling around in the hallway looked shocked, facing the array of weapons. An elevator arrived, and one of the militants forced the occupants into a corner of the hall. The woman, who was standing by the glass doors, opened one and shouted: 'Brother Hassan! Bismillah, no more entries!'

It was nearly five o'clock, and no-one seemed to be trying to enter, in any case.

'Sister Aissa, I hear you,' shouted back one of two coated black men who had produced guns in the main entry, near the steps. The other man with him walked through glass doors into the Classified Advertising section, and began lining up the people there.

Sister Aissa and one of the men stayed in the main reception area, with their guns pointed at the huddled group in the far corner. The rest of the invaders, led by the shavenheaded man, took the elevator that was standing empty. At each floor, a group got off and began screaming orders.

'Bismillah, stand over there! Keep your motherfuckin' hands in the air! Bismillah, anyone move an' I'll blow your fuckin' brains out!' The incongruity of the holy prefatory injunction and the rest of the orders seemed lost on everyone, including the invaders themselves.

At the fifth floor, the leader took a group into the news room, driving before him a few people who were waiting for the elevator. In seconds, the whole area was seized. Editorialists still around at that hour were herded out of their offices and into a space near the archives.

'In the name of God the ever-merciful!' cried the shavenheaded man. 'We are the Wrath of the Messenger. That's our name. I'm Brother Ishak. Do as you're told, and insh'Allah, you'll be safe!'

'Keep your motherfuckin' hands on the desk!' one of his men screamed to an editor who was looking in a drawer for a cigarette.

'Why have we come to the Post?' asked Brother Ishak rhetorically in his powerful voice. 'Because you're a newspaper, and you want the news. Bismillah, we have news to announce! We killed Roger Vishnu Liversedge!' He mouthed the name with hatred.

'Bismillah, *we killed the motherfuckin'*, *ass-lickin' Uncle Tom because for such a motherfuckin'*, *ass-lickin' Uncle Tom to become the first black President of the United States would have been a disgrace! One day, there'll be a real black president in this country, but not Roger Vishnu Liversedge!*' He spat the name out like a curse.

A young man with an M-16 came running in from the elevators.

'Bismillah, *we have the publisher and the executive editor in our hands, Brother Ishak. Shall we put them in chains?*'

The question seemed to have been rhetorical, since Brother Ishak responded in honeyed tones.

'Bismillah, *not if they do as they're told. They too are children of God, the ever-merciful.*'

Brother Ishak turned to the standing group of editors, reporters and morgue staff. A seventeen-year-old black copykid stared back at him in disbelief.

'Bismillah, *you are to replate the front page. I believe that's how you say it*

— replate? Here is your new front page.'
He unfurled a scroll. 'We will stay here
until the papers have gone out. All
editions.'

He thrust the scroll at a tall man of
about forty who was standing near him.
The man looked at the scroll and started,
then half-smiled.

'Bismillah, don't smile, boy!' Brother
Ishak said.

'I'd need the authority of the executive
editor to make the change,' the man said
softly, trying to play for time. 'Or the
publisher.'

'Bismillah, you will give the order. You!
Or the publisher will be thrown out of her
window!' Brother Ishak screamed.

A black reporter said: 'Could some of
us discuss this with you?'

'Ape! White man's monkey! Silence!'
Brother Ishak was either in, or simulat-
ing, a paroxysm of rage. 'Bismillah, I have
spoken. Give the order.' He spoke more
calmly now. 'The printing machines
are in our hands. Every floor is in our
hands.'

'There are laws, sir,' said the tall editor

carefully. 'Is there anything in this — uh — outrageous?'

'Far from it. Far from it, I assure you,' said Brother Ishak.

'All right,' said the editor. 'We will do as you say.'

3

Muir was sitting on the terrace of the old Saint-Georges Hotel, in Beirut, the one that had been destroyed in the fighting in the Seventies, with Doone Kirk of *The Scotsman*, who had been killed during the Vietnamese invasion of Cambodia, and Maha, Doone's Egyptian girlfriend from Alexandria. Mike O'Donnell was improbably there as well, and all of them were telling him that he must write the story at once. It wasn't clear what the story was. He had a bunch of papers on the table, between the coffeecups and the *croissants*, and there was a dab of *confiture d'oranges* on the top page, which bothered him. He was saying that some of the documents were still upstairs, in his room, and he didn't have them all in order. Maha offered to help him with them, saying 'I can read a little Farsi. We lived in Iran when my father worked there.' Now Mike had become Carl, and

Carl was making one of his little academic jokes about the story, throwing in an axiom in classical Greek. 'Hoots, mon,' Kirk was saying, 'you've got to get rrrolling.' He felt rivetted to the chair. Then the papers on the table started blowing away into the street. Now at last he made an effort to spring into action, trying to run after them, but his legs seemed weighted: He was sure he would never get them all, but he must try. Carl said: 'Is that your room up there?' He looked up at the hotel. There were papers blowing from a window. He had to run after the others. Nobody seemed to be helping him, just watching and encouraging him. Papers printed in Farsi were falling into the water where the yachts were moored. He felt desperate, trying to run as though through mud in several directions at once. He awoke.

A light helicopter overhead had caused the dream. It was only just after six. Vuissane was still sleeping. Muir went to the door and got the *Post*. He started, almost dropping the paper. They had, it seemed, left him a different journal by

118

mistake. But no, the masthead was there, and the date was right. Yet the whole of the rest of the front page was in Arabic.

He called the *Post*, asking for whomever was on duty on the national desk. The switchboard operator sounded as though all was normal.

'Thorne,' said a voice.

'Donald Muir.'

'Bill Thorne. We met once at a Harriman party. You probably don't remember me. What can I do for you at this hour?'

'What happened?'

Thorne explained about the raid by the Wrath of the Messenger people.

'Are they still there?'

'No, they gave themselves up to the police after the last edition ran at three-thirty. In fact, we ran it early.'

'They killed Liversedge for being an Uncle Tom?'

'That's what they said.'

'Is everyone okay?'

'Everyone's fine. Did you like our front page?' He was chuckling. 'It's all *suras*, prayers. Beautiful.'

'Very attractive.'

'I think so. I've kept twenty copies.'

Of course. It would be a collector's item.

After he put the receiver down, Muir took the *espresso* machine into the kitchen and turned on the radio softly. The announcer on the first all-news station he tried was saying: 'We have a full sports line-up for this afternoon.' He tried another. Someone was commenting on Gentiluomo, who would be giving a press conference at the White House at eleven. Muir had been anticipating a White House briefing at that hour, presuming it would be held even though this was Saturday. He would certainly go, he decided, if President Gentiluomo was speaking.

The announcer went on: 'Flash! Got a flash item here! The thirty-six black men and one woman who took over *The Washington Post* last night, claiming to be Muslims and to be responsible for the assassination of President Liversedge, are now in custody, and admitted that they had no connection at all to

Liversedge's death.' He paused. He seemed to be paraphrasing an agency despatch. 'The police are inclined to accept their story that they only wanted to publicize their movement, the Wrath of the Messenger.' Another slight pause. 'All of them gave themselves up without a struggle. All had M-16 rifles. If convicted, they face a maximum of twenty years apiece.' Pause. 'The leader, who called himself Brother Ishak, is really Lee Scraper, an unemployed electrician who lives on the 4100 block of Eleventh Street Northeast.'

Muir drank coffee and began to read the *Post*, starting with Page Two. The other papers would arrive shortly.

★   ★   ★

At seven, Liberty arrived to do the cleaning. She was carrying the *Post*. It was the first time he had seen her reading anything not printed on the outside of a cereal box. Muir thought: If the *Post* had known they could increase sales by printing the front page in a foreign language, they'd have done it before.

'You hear the radio?' Liberty asked. She was a heavy, pleasant-looking woman, somewhere around fifty. 'Those dumb people say they kill Roger Liversedge, and he would have been a *good* president.' Muir reflected that what Liberty meant was that Liversedge would have been a *black* president, and a personal friend of her employer's.

'They didn't. It was a prank.'

'A what?'

'A — a joke. I just heard the latest radio bulletin. You must have been in the bus. They apparently wanted publicity for their movement.'

'Pub-lic-i-ty! They go get ten years.'

'Maybe twenty.'

'Ain't that somethin'! They say they Muslims. My son say he Muslim. I say, you get nowhere good without the Lord.'

There was a rustle at the door. Liberty went and brought back *The New York Times*, the morning *Sun* and the *Journal*. Muir spread them on the kitchen table. Liberty put out cereals and began to make weak, American coffee for herself.

Soon, they were reading and eating in an unusual silence.

When Liberty had first come to clean for him some months before, he had asked her if she wanted breakfast. She had said that she had not eaten before she left home, because her 'stomach' was not ready for food in the early morning. Muir had assured her that her stomach wouldn't get the news for a couple of hours, since the food had to go through some formalities in the intestines first.

'Maybe my 'testines not ready,' Liberty had said.

That had set a pattern. From then on, their breakfasts together, three times a week, had become a routine he rarely missed. Liberty had become for him what a favorite taxi driver or hotel room clerk had been when he was a correspondent overseas — his man in the street. But now, for once, she was reversing the input process, and reading what the pundits and the reporters said. For Muir, it was a confirmation that something of moment had happened in America to see Liberty reading *The Wall Street Journal*.

All the papers except the *Post* itself had cast doubts on the black group's claim to guilt. They still had a variety of theories about Liversedge's assassin — white groups, foreign groups angered by the results of some of Liversedge's negotiations, the Mafia (to put Gentiluomo in the White House) or some personal rivals somewhere.

'Liberty, who do you think killed Liversedge?'

'The Klan. If not the Klan, the Nazis. One way or another, some mean white folks. Truth is, I never did quite believe it was those Messenger people, 'spite what they said.'

Her emotion came into play as she translated the killing into words of her own. She put a hand to her mouth to check from crying out in Muir's kitchen. He imagined countless other people across the nation, especially blacks, doing the same, crying for someone they knew only from photographs and brief statements on the tube.

Liberty got up suddenly, collected a duster and furniture polish from a closet and disappeared through the kitchen door. He heard her say: 'Sorry, Miss Wishing.' She had never gotten close to pronouncing Vissuane. 'You sleep on, honey,' she was adding, 'I'll do the bedroom last.' Then he heard her half-sobbing drily and throatily, as she worked. Pushing his cereal plate away, he went out on to the terrace to finish the papers in the morning sun.

He was still, he reflected, not getting much done on the book. The deadline was inching closer, and now New Manhattan Library must be counting on a rigid schedule. Before, being a few weeks or even months late would not have made much difference. Now, a great deal of money was involved. With luck, perhaps he could spend most of the day writing. There was only the White House press conference to worry about, and he certainly wasn't going back to La Niçoise.

* * *

At eight, Raines called.
'Did I wake you?'

'No.'

'Could you come down to my office? A few of us would like to pick your brains on you-know-who's personal relationships.'

'I've got to be at the White House by eleven.'

'Could you come at nine-thirty, then?'

'Sure.'

'We're still tapping your wire. Your front desk has a lot of complaints about you from a man in Wheaton.'

'Abrams?'

'No, I forget the name. He's a Lapp.'

'A what?'

'A Lapp. From Lapland. He said you were stirring up hatred against his people Thursday night. What did you say?'

'Forget it. I'll see you at nine-thirty.'

He could hear Vuissane slip behind him and into the kitchen, then eggs being broken. As he heard the shells go into the sink-disposal, he thought: That's the morning gone, already.

★   ★   ★

Raines asked him to wait before he answered questions, because three other men were going to join them. Muir took the opportunity to put a question himself.

'What are your suspicions?'

'This is on background, right? 'Official source',' Raines said. Muir nodded.

Raines spread his fingers in a protective arch in front of his face. 'First, the Klan,' he went on. 'Second, the Nazis.' Raines was a gray, rather stiff New Englander with a button-down collar, but he sounded strangely like Liberty, theorizing in the kitchen.

The three other men came in together, their grim faces creased in sycophantic smiles. Two were nearly Muir's age, one of them bald, the other with glasses. The third man was younger, with curly hair, and could have been Hispanic.

Raines introduced Muir, and said: 'Don knew Liversedge better than anyone, I think. They went to school together. They were friends. He's been writing a biography of him.'

Muir went on with his own questioning: 'Apart from white groups, who else is suspect?'

'We don't have any actual suspects,' said Raines.

'I mean what other groups would you be thinking about, apart from the Klan and the Nazis.'

'Well, it could be a Palestinian group,' said the curly-haired man, shifting his rump into a more comfortable position in a leather chair. Muir decided he was a Lebanese-American.

'But his Middle East solution had the approval of the PLO,' said Muir. 'They're the government. And he said himself that neither he nor Roberts nor Secretary Grimm solved the Middle East problem, that OPEC did, by getting the message across through the price of oil.'

'One of the splinter groups, perhaps, who weren't satisfied that Israel remains in existence,' the curly-haired man said 'It's obviously a far shot.'

'Yes. Who else.'

'The Zionist Defense Council,' the bald man said. 'They were unhappy with

Liversedge's role in the Israeli withdrawal from the West Bank. They issued a statement about the talks that went on at Camp David this week.'

'Are they the group whose leader is always being arrested in Israel? They've never killed anybody, have they?'

'No, they have goon squads who beat people up, including diplomats, but they've never killed, 'though they've threatened to. They threatened President abu Riad.'

'Would Liversedge be their first target?'

'They're a long shot, too,' the bald man admitted. 'But the ZDC is very irrational. They'd be less likely to think things through than an Arab group, or perhaps I should say more likely to contain a maverick in their midst. And Mr. Liversedge was one of their monsters, because he was always very pro-Palestinian.'

'He was a classic liberal,' Muir said. 'Being a black, liberalism came as part of the rations. And in liberalism, Palestinian rights was always a benchmark: It was one of the things that distinguished the men from the boys.'

'An emotional group wouldn't consider that,' Raines cut in. 'They'd see the Riad-Tewfiq meeting at Camp David as symbolism, and Liversedge's return from the meeting as symbolism, and assassination as symbolism.'

'What other liberal issues of his can you think of, which would have angered foreigners?' The man in glasses was speaking now.

'Independence for the Taiwanese,' said Muir. 'I think he got that idea from his butler, Wong Hwan, who is now the White House butler.'

'That's a thought,' said the bald man, not looking very convinced. 'The Kuo Min Tang would have detested that.'

'You have other foreign groups in mind, yourselves?'

'The South Africans,' said Raines. 'Their hit squads have murdered a lot of blacks overseas, although always their own people, including some in the United States. They have a revolution going on out there, of course; they wouldn't want a black president in the United States. You have to say to yourself: These people are irrationals, emotionals, they have a background of holding human life cheap. Anyway, we're checking that direction, too.'

'Anyone else?' asked Muir.

'The Puerto Rican independence movement. They're not foreign, of course, but Liversedge spoke out against them.' It was the bald man speaking again. 'Or a Greek-American group which thought he went too far when he mediated the partition of Cyprus into two sovereign states.'

'Greece accepted it.'

'Some Greek Americans are more Greek than the Greeks.'

'Who else?'

'Turks, dissatisfied with the final size of independent Kibris. I guess we tended to throw that in because there are so many Greek extremists on the other side,' the bald man said.

'Why not the Armenians?' Muir was smiling, in spite of the gravity of the subject.

The man in glasses smiled also. 'Yes,

they once threatened him too.'

Raines said: 'He got about seventy death threats a year. That's low for a vice president. Some were repeats, of course, not seventy different people. We're trying to bring in every kook who ever said at a party: I'd like to kill the black sonovabitch. Believe me, we're working. We're even checking to see if he ever annoyed the IRA. Wouldn't that be far out, for a black veep? After all, they *are* killers. But tell us about his private life. Who were his enemies? Go back to the early days. We've got to be thorough.'

'I can't think, right off, of anything useful about his childhood or at college,' Muir said. 'He was a pretty reserved guy. He used to say that he had never experienced much racial discrimination in his life, but you could see it was because he never went looking for it. And he was light-skinned, usually well-dressed, well-spoken.'

'Beyond race?' asked Raines.

'Nothing I know of.'

'His family — there is only a sister.'

'Yes. She lives in Newport. She's down

here now for the funeral.'

'He must have had enemies in politics.'

'Rivals, certainly; but he never mentioned having a real knockdown-dragout with anybody, even in his campaign for governor. He was a helluva compromiser.'

'He was also a prosecutor.'

'Yes, he sent a lot of people up, of course; but that would mean someone carrying a grievance for a long time. He was state attorney general. As governor, he turned down some pardons. But would anyone suddenly do it for that reason at that particular time? It would have been less difficult to get him before. It just doesn't sound like a personal thing.'

'That's the heart of the problem,' said the bald man. 'Whoever did it presumably did it because Mr. Liversedge was about to become President, or rather because he had just become President. Within about an hour, someone had to make the decision, plan the whole thing, get the weapon, decide on the right spot, and do it. To begin with, the person had to get the news as soon as it went out on the radio — about Roberts' death, and Liversedge returning by helicopter.'

'By the way,' said Muir. 'Two guys from your explosives division were round at my place yesterday morning, asking me the color of the flames and that sort of thing. Have you found a weapon?'

Raines and the others exchanged glances.

'This is sensitive, Don,' Raines said. 'May I go on deep background?'

'Sure.'

'We've reason to believe that the Director will be making a statement later this morning about a weapon. On deep background, we have recovered it. Near the bridge over Rock Creek, by the Thompson Boathouse.'

'Your explosives people said it was a missile launcher,' said Muir. They hadn't gone that far, but he was probing for Raines to tell him more.

The FBI men exchanged glances again, and Raines said: 'I don't want to go into details until the Director has made a statement, and I don't know for sure what he plans to do.'

'It certainly looked like a small missile shot,' Muir said. 'If the killer left behind a disposable launcher, there would be prints.'

'On deep background again, I'll tell you this much: We recovered the gloves.'

'So there were no prints. The gloves must have been very fine.'

'They were plastic — kitchen gloves, the sort your cleaner probably uses for washing up.'

'Let's get back to Mr. Liversedge,' said the man with glasses. 'Did you ever hear reports that he might have been a homosexual?'

'Yes. I tried to check that out. He had a manner that could have been seen by some as a little effete, but he had no close relationship with men that I could discover. Of course, if that rumor had been true, he would have to have been bisexual. He had a long attachment to a Korean girl, during the war, and the only time he nearly married, according to what he told me, the woman was a Japanese-American who taught at the Rhode Island

School of Design.'

'No jealous husbands?' asked the bald man.

'None that I heard of,' Muir said. 'I'm still thinking of the circumstances — the sudden decision, the whole plan devised and enacted within an hour. It doesn't suggest someone who had been gunning for him for years. Did some of those seventy annual threats of yours come from people who knew him personally?'

'It's hard to say,' said Raines. 'None of them, according to our computer, used phraseology which suggested that they knew him closely.'

'Did he discuss his overseas negotiations with you, in connection with your book?' asked the man with curly hair.

'Yes.'

'I'm just wondering if the killing was connected to the Camp David thing, as we mentioned before, the new Palestinian state, something like that, and if it was only a coincidence that he became President on the night of the murder. If so, it could have taken more than an hour to plan.' He was thinking aloud. There didn't seem to be a question for Muir to answer.

Muir said: 'I'm not being much help. Perhaps if I re-read my book — most of it is written — and perhaps looked at some of the notes, to see if they suggest anything.'

'Sex,' the bald man cut in, suddenly. He was looking down, reflectively, and taking no apparent notice of Muir's last remarks. 'If it was a private execution, that usually means money or sex,' he said.

'He took more of a vicarious interest in other people's sex lives than he seemed to do in his own,' said Muir.

'Oh really, what do you mean?' asked the bald official.

'Well, when he was attorney general of Rhode Island, he used to ride shotgun for Governor Irwin in those matters. Irwin was balling a minor clerk in his office, and because she was black he asked Liversedge to make the arrangements.'

'It may not be relevant, and Irwin's dead, but I'm fascinated,' said the man with glasses. 'Tell us more.'

'Liversedge would pretend that he was

giving her a ride home sometimes, because she had no car. He said he knew her father. It was a device. Liversedge would drive her to his own house, where he lived alone, and the governor would come by later.'

'So much for New England morality,' said the curly-haired man, grinning at Raines. 'And to think he was the goddam attorney general.'

'Did he ever — uh — ponce for anyone else?' asked Raines.

'Well, I don't think he thought of it as — '

'I'm kidding,' said Raines. 'You know what I mean.'

'Well, he might have. He had a lot of stories about what went on in party conventions. Either he just liked to collect gossip, or — no, I think he had personal knowledge of some of those things. In fact, I know he did.'

'Let me put this to you frankly,' said the bald man. 'Obviously, Liversedge, as the Wrath of the Messenger people said, licked a lot of white ass to get where he got. Did he fix any party bigwigs up with black girls?' The question sounded as much prurient as forensic.

'He never told me. If he did, he'd have been more vulnerable to blackmail, as President, than the people he fixed. But it wouldn't have been impossible.'

'Of course not.'

'I mean, I wouldn't have been utterly startled if he had. It was his one incongruity — the childish fun he seemed to get out of other people's sexual peccadillos. I think he would have found it amusing to think of Senator X perorating about declining family stan-dards, while also thinking of him holed up in a Cranston hotel with a semi-literate waitress. I don't think he would have had any phony hang-ups about it being degrading to the 'race'. He was a patrician sort of guy, as you know, yet he dearly liked locker-room stories. But that doesn't help much, does it?'

There was a pause. Muir looked at his watch.

'Hank,' said Raines to the curly-headed man. 'Do you still have anything else on the political-motive line?'

'I guess not, right now,' said Hank.

'Paul, anything more?' He was looking at the man in glasses.

'Only that if Mr. Muir finds something in his book or his notes, we'd be grateful for any tip. All we have is a weapon — that's deep background, of course, until the statement comes out.'

'Gene?'

The bald man rubbed his eyes with the palm of a hand and said: 'I think he was killed by a Nazi or a Kluxer or some lonely nut with Nazi or Kluxer views, but I can't prove it.' He made a last stab in another direction: 'Did he ever do an interview with *Playboy* or *Penthouse*?'

'No,' said Muir. He remembered why Liversedge had turned them both down: He had been afraid that he might tell too many stories.

He hesitated, about to get up and leave. 'There's one more thing I should perhaps say,' he said, looking at Raines. 'As you know, I witnessed the crash — the explosion. And I also saw a man running away.'

'Didn't you tell the police?' asked

Raines. All four of them were staring at him.

'No.'

'Why not?'

'Well, there was another eye-witness on the ground — I was on my balcony — and he was telling the police about the person running away and pointing in the direction in which the person ran. I figured he had had a closer look than I had, and I didn't want to spend all night just corroborating what he — and the people in the second helicopter — said. I knew I had a busy day in front of me.'

'Don, I'm astounded,' Raines said. 'You really should have told the police.'

'I guess I should. I'm telling you now.'

'You must have noticed that we've said nothing about a person being seen running away. The witness has been discreet. We don't want the killer to know that someone saw a figure in flight. How did the person look to you?'

'Small. Short hair.'

'Like mine?' asked the curly-haired man, running his fingers through his own.

'No. Sort of smooth.'

'Stocky?' asked the bald man.

'No, thin.'

'Age?'

'No idea. Not too old to run. I never saw a face.'

'He ran off in what direction?'

'He or she ran off under the Whitehurst Freeway.'

'You say he or she,' said the man in glasses. 'Do you have any reasons to think it might have been a woman?'

Muir hesitated, wishing he hadn't used the feminine pronoun. Raines gave him a little negative shake of the head. He apparently wanted Muir to keep the restaurant operation discreet, and was holding it back for some reason from at least one of his colleagues. Muir was glad that he was not on a lie-detector test. 'Not really,' he said. Was that misprision of something? A felony? Oh well, Raines knew about the first non-encounter, and Miss No-Name had said that she would give herself up; it would only be with his cooperation if they caught her at all — if she was telling the truth, of course.

'Wearing pants, I presume,' said

Raines, coming to his rescue.

'Yes.'

'That doesn't tell us much. No feminine curves?' asked the bald man.

'No. It certainly wasn't a buxom woman, if it was a woman.'

'Anything else?' asked Raines. 'You didn't see color of clothes, or whatever?'

'Not in the lamplight.'

'Carry anything?'

'No.'

'It matches the other description,' said the man in glasses.

★ ★ ★

The press room in the west wing of the White House was full. Muir reflected that they should have used the auditorium in the Executive Office Building next door, but probably Gentiluomo wanted the famous setting.

'This is the last train from Paris,' a television reporter was saying to his crew, going through the usual exercise of limbering himself up verbally before the daily attack on the spokesman began.

'I can't believe Gentiluomo will keep Packer on as his press secretary,' Brad Williams was saying to Muir. 'Did you see much of him on the Hill?'

'Packer's over the hill,' quipped Muir, weakly.

The buzz of voices died as Reeves appeared, followed by Packer. Field Reeves had been Roberts' press secretary and he was staying on for a few days to help with the transition. The TV lights went on as Reeves reached the lectern.

'Just two announcements,' Reeves said. 'Firstly, the two presidents will lie in state and on view to the public from seven p.m. in the Rotunda. The press can go in at six, and photographers have pretty much free range. After seven, only two pool photographers will be permitted, because of the limited space, to shoot the crowds filing past the — uh — bodies.

'Second, President Gentiluomo has been informed by FBI Director Stafford that the weapon that was used to kill President Liversedge has been recovered and identified. I understand Mr. Stafford is giving a press conference at twelve.'

'Is there a State Department briefing today?' a reporter was asking those around him quietly. That would normally be at twelve also. There was a whispered chorus of negatives.

'President Gentiluomo will be here in about ten minutes,' Reeves said. 'Any questions on those two points?'

Reeves' angular features under bushy gray hair looked authoritative and, as usual, impatient, as though any request for questions could only bring trouble. Beside him, Packer, a bulky man of sixty-eight with a drinker's face, seemed almost expressionless, except when he occasionally smiled at faces he recognized.

'When will President Gentiluomo come to the Rotunda?' an agency reporter asked.

'Thank you for reminding me,' Reeves said, glancing quickly at Packer, as though Packer should have thought of that. 'Six-fifteen, I think. Isn't that right?' Packer nodded. 'Anything else on the Rotunda?'

There was a hiatus, and a woman reporter asked: 'Were there any prints on the weapon?' The voice was light, and Reeves' stenographer looked up questioningly.

'The question was asked as to whether there were any prints found on the weapon,' Reeves said. 'You'll have to ask Mr. Stafford that, Jenny.'

'Who found the weapon — the D.C. Police?'

'You'll have to ask Mr. Stafford that.'

'Can you answer any questions about the weapon?' asked Williams.

'Frankly, no, Brad,' Reeves said. 'Mr. Stafford has the details, and he knows what he can tell you.'

'Do the police or the FBI have any suspects?'

'Again, that's for Mr. Stafford, John.'

'May I ask you,' another reporter said, 'if the White House will ask the Director to make concrete responses to questions like these?' Reeves ignored him. There was more in this fruitless vein until Gentiluomo arrived. He was a short, jockey-sized man with thin white hair, who had represented the same Connecticut district for thirty-two years. He was supposed to have had Mafia ties in his early terms, but now it was commonly believed that he no longer needed their help in getting re-elected, and that he held the Mob at arm's length; but Liversedge's death had revived old rumors. As he came in, more TV strobes came on, and there was a new tension in the room. Packer half-shuffled to the lectern and proclaimed hoarsely: 'Ladies and gentlemen, the President of the United States.' The few reporters who had found seats stood up.

Gentiluomo blinked in the lights. He already seemed five years older than a few days before. A normally aggressive, bantamcock of a man, he now looked genuinely humble.

'Thank you, Dick,' he said, putting a prepared text on the lectern. 'Be seated, everyone.' There were few seats available, and no-one sat. He cleared his throat and paused.

'My friends, I knew Henry Roberts for a great many years, as a congressman, as a senator, as a great president and a great leader of our party. I was shocked by his premature death, as I know everyone was, and I wish again to extend my deepest condolences to Ellen Roberts and the family. The American people have lost a true leader. I dedicate myself today to preserving his memory by fighting for his legislative program, and I hope my friends on Capitol Hill will continue to work with me as they have done in the past.'

'Meaning, he'll succeed with legislation where Roberts didn't,' Williams whispered to Muir sardonically.

Gentiluomo went on: 'I have known Roger Liversedge for the past three years. As President of the Senate, the Vice President was of course my opposite number in the other House of Congress, and he became a good friend and a valued colleague. But for the monstrous events of early Friday morning, he would, I'm sure, have been a fine president. The first single task of my administration will be to find who was responsible for his assassination and to bring that person or persons to trial.'

He looked up from the lectern and into the cameras. He was striving for the right expression of grief, sincerity, commitment.

'Friends, it is said that some of us are born great and that some of us have greatness thrust upon us. I told one of you many years ago that the dream of my life was to be Speaker of the House, and when that dream was achieved, I believed that what years I still had to give to my country — as you know, I'll be seventy-one next month — would be in that office. It was not to be.

'It is said that history is not made by men, but that men ride its currents and either succeed or fail.' Muir felt sure the President must have gotten that quotation wrong. How could people not make history? Probably Packer's fault. Muir looked at Williams quizzically, but Williams stared straight ahead, seemingly now beguiled by the historic nature of the moment. Gentiluomo went on: 'For the nineteen months that I will hold this office, I will strive not to fail. I will need the help of all the American people, and I ask you, ladies and gentlemen, to help me, too, in this intimidating task which has been thrust upon me.' He paused. 'I'll take questions.'

The questions were mostly about particular elements of policy, about his priorities in the domestic program. The first question was the only one that drew much general interest: Had he chosen a vice president?

'I would like to give that a lot of thought,' said the little figure. The interest died. Gentiluomo was not making much of an impact.

After five minutes or so of questions, Muir looked at his watch. It was just past eleven-thirty. He had decided that he would return to the Niçoise after all. What did he have to lose? If she turned up and he didn't, he might be missing the biggest story of his life, incredible as her explanations had sounded so far.

'See you,' he said to Williams. 'I have an appointment.'

4

He was on time. The maître d'hôtel showed him to a table.

'Alone?'

'Two. I'm expecting someone.' Now, if she didn't come for the second time, he would feel foolish.

A waiter roller-skated toward the table.

'*Un apéritif, monsieur?*'

'Campari-soda.'

'*Tout de suite, monsieur.*'

A few minutes later, a short young woman with a suntanned face and large, fierce-red lips came in. She turned to speak quietly to the maître d'hôtel. She wore her bobbed, tightly-combed, shining hair in a ducktail. The maître d'hôtel pointed to Muir and began to bring her over. He wore that smile with which maîtres d'hôtel bring girls to the tables of waiting men. Muir stood up. She glanced down until she was almost upon him: He guessed she was shortsighted.

How should he greet her? He held out both arms to take her hand. She threw up both of hers and embraced him.

'Donald! You look wonderful!' She was playing the role of an old friend. She bussed his cheek and he bussed hers. They sat, and she kleenexed the lipstick off his face.

The maître d'hôtel was beaming. 'A drink, madame?'

'An old-fashioned. For an old-fashioned girl!'

There seemed to be no mistaking her elation. Muir found himself smiling at her dumbly, unsure how to begin the conversation. She had said that she was pretty, and she certainly was. Except for her height — about five feet — she had the body of a model. He doubted if she weighed more than ninety pounds. Blood-red shoes matched both her lips and the casual velours sash around her white lace dress. She certainly made a good partner to be seen lunching with. What would Vuissane say, if she knew? And this was his most important interview, ever? This was Roger's killer?

There was an awkward silence between them until the drinks came. Then, they clinked glasses.

'To your Pulitzer,' she said. That was what Duane Smith had said, lifting a scotch-sour after offering him the White House job. But her thought seemed more generous, less egoistic, if only because of the unlikelihood of her expectation, compared to Smith's.

'To your survival,' he said. He could think of no other realistic wish, in her case.

She gave a smirk. 'They always give my sort of people the maximum, and you know what that is. Let's talk of something else. I'll tell you everything afterward, when we get home.'

'When did you start listening to the show?' Muir asked.

'Six months ago.' She took a heavy slug from her drink. 'I like your choice of music; but even more, I like your mind, your humor. You're different. But most of all, it's your voice.'

'It's the only one I've got.'

'I like to fantasize that it's all mine. But

I know there are over three times as many single or available women in Washington as there are men, and you guys get hassled.'

'Not if you stay away from bus stops and the Georgetown Safeway,' Muir said. 'You can usually hold your own at parties.' She giggled.

The waiter had skated up again and was asking them if they wanted to order.

'Steak tartare,' she said. 'I like raw meat.'

'A cannibal's breakfast,' echoed the waiter. One of the restaurant's characteristics was waiter-humor.

'Make it two cannibals' breakfasts,' said Muir, 'and a carafe of red wine.' The waiter jotted it down, and skated off.

'What do you do, apart from listening to my show?'

'I'm a witch.'

This came with a short, teasing laugh.

'You have a magic wand?'

'I have a magic vulva.' Despite the provocative remark, her face became serious, almost thoughtful.

Later, he watched her eat: She did it

with almost sexual gluttony. The big red mouth devoured the plate of red meat, constantly adding more black pepper, more mustard; when she drank wine, it was like a perspiring tennis player drinking Coca-Cola. He could feel the enormous sensuality of this little woman in virtually everything she did. Good grief, thought Muir, I think this kid really is in love with my voice.

But what really mattered, in any event, was not the depth of her attraction but the story that she had to give. Muir found himself constantly switching, in his mind, between a sense of expectancy about her promised confession and a sense of outraged absurdity that he was actually there, having a friendly lunch with her; or between anticipation over her exuberant libido, which began to envelop the table like perfume from a Hindu legend, and his purposely muted outrage that she had actually fired the missile into Roger's plane. He was surprised that the monstrous ambivalence of it all didn't take away his appetite, which seemed to keep in step with his curiosity. He was eating, like her, as though he had nothing else in mind but lunch.

She seemed confident and satisfied. There was certainly no outward indication that she was as unbalanced as the murder itself implied, except her seeming ability to dismiss, at will, the very thought of retribution. There had to be other reasons, Muir decided, why she had murdered Roger. Had she known Roger personally? His sexual life had always been as discreet as his interest in the sexual life of others had been prurient. Muir felt frustrated by his promise not to discuss the killing until they reached her home. The questions that her presence posed grew more numerous all the time. How much of the book would have to be rewritten if it turned out that she had known Liversedge for several years before she murdered him? Had she been a frequent, secret visitor to Admiral's House? She didn't seem like Roger's type — too vulgar. But who knew? Carl's deadline looked more and more improbable at the thought of the ramifications which the woman's very mystery already presented.

After the raw meat and wine, they drank two strong coffees. She chattered about Washington, about jazz, about a movie which she had seen the week before. Her relaxed manner seemed totally inappropriate. The crimson mouth moved constantly in the almost unlined face, which bore no traces of any great emotion, present or past. She didn't even have the fleshiness of features which he normally associated with self-indulgence. He found himself fascinated — and surprised at his own fascination. Finally, she said: 'Now we'll go home for an afternoon you shall never forget. And I shall never forget, for what time I have left. I've made love to other men, Donald, and thought of you. And now it will be you, at last. And when you're resting, I'll bring you wine and the most exclusive story you ever heard.'

'Where do you live?'

'Kensington.'

'Kensington?' The dull suburb seemed inappropriate, after her heavy-handed promises of eroticism. It was as though she had said that Nirvana was a district in downtown Cleveland, or that the Garden of Delights was hidden in the northern Bronx.

'It *is* rather a long way. Do you have a car? No, I have an idea. There's a Holiday Inn just up the street, a couple of blocks or so. We could walk there. Shall we?'

'Sure.'

★　★　★

He had barely tipped the porter for not smiling at their luggagelessness before she was beginning to peel off her dress. As the door closed, she had nothing left on but her panties and a necklace. As he undressed, she went through exercises, watching her lithe body in a mirror. She seemed to enjoy the sight of it as much as men undoubtedly did. Muir reflected that he had been prepared to pay an unusual price to find out how his friend had died; but he felt slightly guilty now that it was a price that he would not mind disbursing. But then again, only slightly guilty — after all, the whole thing was a story which Roger would have enjoyed telling, if he had been around to do so. In a way, the ghastly joke was on Roger in a way that only Roger might have appreciated to the full.

She lay on the bed and stared at his own nakedness. He found himself staring at her in return. The small head and the short hair only emphasized her body. It was, now he thought of it, exactly the figure in slacks and shirt which he had seen running from Thompson's parking lot. Slim as she was, she did move rather like a man. He put the parking-lot scene out of his mind as best he could. She had tiny breasts, he noted, but the nipples were the largest he had ever seen.

'I've never slept with a witch before,' he said, as he lay down beside her. It was galling how few things one could find to say on occasions like this, even if you were a phrasemaker by profession; he understood why he and Vuissane preferred their silences.

'I knew you were big by the depth of your voice,' she said.

159

'You said you'd seen me leaving the studio.'

'I'm not talking about your height, you noodle! I'm talking about your length.'

He kissed her nipples, feeling them rise like hard blossoms in his mouth. But she soon tired of such preliminaries.

'Donald, I'm hot, hot! Lie back.'

The less-than-lifesize sculpture was straddling him and beginning to make barely perceptible movements. Almost at once, she was gasping.

'Oh! Oh!'

He was startled by the incredible speed with which she had come to climax. Could it be for real? Her head went back. 'Aah!'

Then, she lowered her head forward, holding on to his belly for support. Suddenly, she leaned over and kissed him wetly. He found himself responding to her kiss.

She drew herself up slowly; this time, with even less movement on her part, she was ecstasizing again. There were the same cries; the head went back. 'Aah! My god!' Then, the huge nipples were bearing down, and there was the same grateful kiss. Then again, gripping his solar plexus, she swung slowly back upright. Her head gave an involuntary shake and she was once again orgiastic. Muir watched her with bemused curiosity, almost admiration, the first nymphomaniac he had ever known.

After the seventh time, he lost count. After all, he told himself glibly, I'm a reporter, not a Guinness editor. Finally, she climaxed less intensely, and as she kissed him she said: 'Come when you want.'

'I want,' he said, raising his knees behind her tiny stern.

When he had reached his climax, he relaxed, but only for a few seconds. He could feel the lips of her vulva stirring themselves around him in a washing motion, keeping him erect. Half a minute later, he came once more. Then again. After the fourth time, she let him subside.

★   ★   ★

161

She was lying on him, lazily nuzzling his neck.

'That was beautiful,' he said. He felt, in some perverse gentlemanly way, that he owed her that.

'I told you that you would remember.' There was self-satisfaction in her tone, a sort of childish boastfulness which he couldn't help but like.

'Don't I get to know your name now?'

'Uh-uh. Miss No-Name. Or Mrs. No-Name, to be honest.'

'But I'll have to have your name in the story.'

She did not respond. After a while, she eased herself off him gently and went to the bathroom. He heard the shower. He leaned over to his jacket, lying on a chair, and extracted his notebook and a pen. He put them on the bedside table and lay back again, waiting.

She came in, still slightly wet, still naked.

'I promised you wine, and there is none,' she said, teasingly.

'And you promised a story.' Now, it had to come to that. No-Name had said she was going to talk herself into the electric chair. Would she break down?

'And there is none,' she said.

She gave a little teasing laugh again, at his puzzlement. 'Donald, how old are you?'

He lied a little: 'Forty-five.'

'Aren't you a little mature to be still believing in witches?'

She kissed him again, but he felt too foolish to respond. Instead, he said: 'Why did you take such a ridiculous risk? — the telephone calls, coming to the restaurant — you could have been picked up by the FBI.'

'I guessed you'd tell someone, and they'd be watching you. But I haven't committed any offense. I didn't force you here, did I?'

She began putting on her clothes, with a glance at her watch. She gave a half-giggle.

'Did you really see me walking around with a cannon, or whatever it was?'

She sat on the bed, leaned down and kissed him goodbye. He kissed her back, recognizing her victory, glad after all that she had not murdered his friend, the President. He was almost surprised to find that the knowledge that he had been made into an idiot, that there was no story after all, was a relief.

'I may call you again. I'm sorry about the story. But I was good, wasn't I?'

'No complaints,' he said.

The little head went back, and she was laughing teasingly again.

'I *love* that. 'No complaints.' Say it for me on the show. Say it — you'll find a way — at the end, on Monday night. Now, I have to fly. I have to get home and prepare my husband's dinner.'

'You're kidding.'

'No, I really am a good cook,' she said.

He found himself staring at the door after she had gone.

★　★　★

When Muir returned to the Watergate, the Ethiopian clerk on duty at that time of the day handed him his message slips. One asked him to call 'Mr. Manes.' Was it the clerk's misunderstanding, or was

164

Raines just being especially discreet? Upstairs, he called the FBI number. Raines came to the point without bothering with amenities.

'Don, I'd like to talk to you again.' He added, in matter-of-fact tones: 'I gather the woman caller never reappeared.' It sounded more like an assumption than a question, and Muir said nothing. 'There's something a little — uh — harder I'd like to share with you.'

'Fine.'

'May I come to your place?'

'Of course.'

'I'll be there in about fifteen minutes. Is that okay?'

'Sure.'

After he put the receiver down, Muir felt nervous. His session with Mrs. No-Name, on top of lunch, had left him feeling soporific. The effort to concentrate on what was presumably going to be a serious conversation with Raines, who was now his most important cooperative source, made him suddenly wish that the story would go away for a while. He went to the bathroom and washed his face with cold water. He used eye lotion. He still felt half-sedated. He looked at himself in disgust in the bathroom mirror: He didn't, he decided, look at all like the reporter who was going to be the first with the story of the decade; he looked, he thought, like one of Raines' gray-faced colleagues, grimly collecting time in the bureaucracy.

Raines, when he arrived, also did not look like Efrem Zimbalist in one of the Bureau's finer moments. He resembled a man with a big fish, somewhere out there, on a frazzled line, uncertain how to get it aboard.

He walked in, glancing around at the pictures on the walls from India, Iran and China, the African masks, the hanging carpet from Kazakstan, the signed photographs of Arafat and a dead Kurdish general, taken by a photographer who had died at Muir's side in Viet Nam. He had never been in Muir's home before, and it probably looked very different from his own. Though he and Raines had always gotten along well in their slightly adversary relationship, Muir suspected that Raines was now nervous to have a reporter as a collaborator.

'Nice view,' Raines said mechanically, looking out at the Potomac.

'Beer? Coffee?'

'Do you have scotch?'

'Sure. How d'you like it?'

While Muir fixed the scotch, Raines sat uneasily in an easy chair, saying nothing. He was obviously concentrating on how much he could say and how much he couldn't. The arc of his fingers went into the protective pose in front of his face, like a flying buttress supporting a rather craggy cathedral which had seen better days. Muir sat down, nursing a glass of water. Raines raised his scotch quickly, sipped fast, and put the glass down on a side table clumsily, making a noise.

'What I have to tell you is still on deep background,' he said. 'But I promise you it will not go to anyone else until after I've given you my release.' The terminology was odd. 'You'll be first, you know what I mean?' Muir nodded, waiting to learn what his quid pro quo would have to be.

Raines went on: 'One government,

more than any other, was desperately opposed from the start to Roger Liversedge's selection as vice president, and precisely because of the fear that Roberts might die in office. They would have seen any black person becoming President of the United States as a disaster.'

'South Africa?'

'Right.'

'It could have proved to their advantage,' Muir said. 'They could have figured that Liversedge would have had to be just a fraction more patient with Pretoria than Roberts, to show that he wasn't putting his ethos before America's national interest. And, judging from his career, they should have thought that that would be the line that he would probably follow.'

'Are you sure?'

'I'm not saying that's how he would have been. I'm saying that you don't get to be governor of Rhode Island because you're black, but in spite of it.'

'Right. But the very fact that he was black was like a red light to them, if you'll forgive the mixed metaphor.'

They both smiled, and Raines seemed to relax a little.

'Actually, Roger would have been bad news for South Africa in the presidency,' Muir said. 'But what are your facts?'

'I'll tell you what we know, or some of what we know. Then I would like you to tell me anything that you can that confirms or infirms our line.'

The quid pro quo seemed reasonable. It was no more than Raines had implicitly asked before. Muir said: 'Go ahead.'

Raines had been creeping forward on his chair as he spoke, his normally Ivy League manner sliding into something close to excitement or animation. Now he sat back again, and the nave of slim fingers slipped like a mask across his features once more.

'As you know, the South African government has done a number of free-wheeling things in this country, going back to the 'Sixties. Things like trying to buy the Washington *Star*, junkets and slush funds for Congressmen and others, procuring sophisticated U.S. weapons denied to them by the Office of

169

Munitions Control under the embargo. As I mentioned at the office, they have hit men in America who have made some of the exile leaders from South Africa disappear. A former president of the student union out there is now at the bottom of Lake Michigan. A Zulu fashion model in Chicago who was a courier for the black nationalists died of an overdose of barbiturates, but the coroner was wrong — it wasn't suicide or voluntary drug abuse. The exiled editor of a South African paper, I forget the paper's name but the man's name was Campbell — you probably remember the case — was killed in a car crash last year in upstate New York. I can tell you that the brake lines had been tampered with so that any time he really put the brakes on hard, they would snap. We've kept most of this out of the press because the case is hard to put together. We wanted a conviction.'

Muir nodded. 'All those were South African citizens, I presume.'

'That's right. But the guy who runs their outfit here is ruthless, and he has a cache of arms in his home.'

'I hope you have him bugged.'

Raines ignored the remark, saying instead: 'We know that he is the author or originator of at least one threatening letter to Liversedge, telling him, in effect, to watch his tongue on South Africa or else. He had made it look as though the writer were American — even had it sent from Biloxi, Mississippi.'

'How long have you known he was the author?'

'Since just before I called you, just now. We've been through his place and we have his typewriter.'

'Why didn't Roger go public with the letter at the time he received it?'

'The Secret Service advised him not to — it might have given others the same idea. We almost never go public with threats against the President or the Vice President.'

'What's the guy's name?'

'That I can't tell you now, but I will when I give you my release.'

'What does he do — I mean, officially?'

Raines shook his head. 'All I can say right now is that he lives in Washington, that he left his apartment shortly before the assassination, carrying a soft weekend bag, and returned shortly afterward. The bag then appeared to be empty.'

'When did you learn that?'

'Late this morning.'

'You think he did it himself?'

'Probably. His hit men are mostly students — black stooges, people with relatives back home in South Africa. He may have felt they'd be frightened to do this one, that they'd get caught and talk, or whatever.'

'Is he under arrest?'

Raines buried his face in his hands. 'We can't find him,' he said. He looked up. 'It was a neighbor who saw his going and coming on Thursday night. The guy's been missing since. The place where he works says he's on vacation, they don't know where.'

'How can I help?'

'Tell me all you can think of about Mr. Liversedge and South Africa.'

'He was invited there once.'

'I remember.'

'That was over two years ago. He sort

of put it off. He told me he was tempted to go, out of curiosity, but that he thought he would be so restricted in what he could say to audiences there that Pretoria would be able to use his visit to their advantage.'

'Who talked to him about this?'

'The South African ambassador.'

'He made a formal call?'

'Yes.'

'Any follow-up?'

'Yes, a senior embassy official later called at Roger's office with some details of the proposed trip, which Roger had asked for.'

'Then, what?'

'Oh, he just put it off. Never actually said 'no', in case a visit might turn out to have some advantage for the Administration, but never setting any tentative date.'

'Do you know what their reaction was — the South Africans?'

'They were miffed, of course. I guess he became more suspect to them then. They said his predecessor had gone.'

Raines nodded. 'Now tell me, Don. You knew Liversedge so well. What were his feelings about South Africa? Just disapproval? I know he liked to present an image of not putting his blackness forward, but — '

'He was outraged.'

Raines' features loosened. 'He didn't strike any of us as a man who outraged easily. A slow fuse.'

'He *did* have a very slow fuse,' said Muir, 'but he saw South Africa as the incarnation of political evil. He equated it with Nazi Germany, and he couldn't understand why most Americans hesitated to draw quite that parallel. Frankly, I agreed with him. It wasn't empathy for the black peasant or the black slum dweller: He had no way of knowing how somebody like that felt. He was outraged as a sophisticated American, concerned about U.S. policy. I don't know that his own color had much to do with it.'

'You did say something about how his attitude to South Africa, if he had been in the White House, would not have been altogether low-key. I take it he talked about this with you, over the years?'

174

'Not much, over the years, but in recent months, to do with the book. We talked about his agreement not to run for the presidency, and this led naturally to talking of what he would have wanted to do if he *had* become President.'

'And he talked about South Africa in that context?'

Muir paused a moment, intrigued to have reversed roles with Raines. He had been filling a pipe while he talked, and now it needed lighting. When it was drawing well, he said: 'That would have been one of his most dramatic projects — in fact, almost none of the others were really dramatic, because drama really wasn't his style; and he believed that most reforms, in foreign or any policy, should be slow in order to be lasting.'

He picked a tamper up from a side table and flattened the loose ash in the bowl of his pipe before going on.

'He would have intended, very early in his Administration, to make a statement on South Africa, putting everything in context — morals, U.S. interests, defense, economics. He had laid it all out in his mind like a legal argument, leading to one inexorable conclusion: That the South African regime had to go, and that the U.S. could not be perceived to be wrong on this issue while the Soviet Union was right. The climax of his statement would have been his announcement that he was breaking relations with Pretoria and calling — at the U.N. — for an oil embargo on the country. You can guess what would have happened: Most of the oil-producing countries are in the Third World and they couldn't be upstaged by the United States on a question like this. He was even prepared to have U.S. ships fly the U.N. flag to implement such a resolution.

'As Roger saw it, it would bring the revolution to rapid victory, end the fighting, save bloodshed, and put the United States in the position of being the new government's best friend, even if the new government was Marxist. He figured a Marxist government using Soviet weapons to come to power would be looking to put some distance between itself and Moscow, and would want U.S.

technicians to keep its industries and everything going.'

Raines looked satisfied. 'That's what we call a motive,' he said.

Muir drew on his pipe. 'You think the South Africans knew all this, and feared he might become president — that they had Liversedge's office bugged?'

'We know they had it bugged. We removed the bugs yesterday.'

'How do you know the bugs were South African?'

'We know who put them in.'

'You mean he was one of yours — a double agent?'

'Not quite,' said Raines, finally permitting a smile on his strained features, 'otherwise we would have known about his policy plans — what you've just told me.' The nave of fingers came down and he reached for his glass. 'But you're warm. Anyway, we know they bugged him — and, of course, on the occasions you have mentioned, you.'

★　★　★

He watched Raines drive off in a light shower. The nervous bureaucrat seemed confident that he had found the inside track in the investigation. If Raines kept his word, there might be some way that Muir could be the first with the news, but that was doubtful. He was tied to his program time, and to the fact that he would not have an audience again until Monday evening. But his principal interest was in the development itself, rather than in how news of it first reached the public. The fact of a foreign government being responsible for the death of a U.S. president had made the book even more compelling, even if he had to go to print before the trial. But, Muir wondered, did it put his own life at risk, since he had known Roger's intentions with regard to South Africa — the evidence as to why South Africa had had him killed?

He called the front desk downstairs, which had been taking his calls while Raines was there. It was now a female voice that answered.

'Mr. Muir,' she said, 'you had a

succession of kook calls, seven in all, and one from a Mr. Olutunde at the Nigerian Embassy. D'you want his number?'

'Please.' What was an African diplomat doing, calling him on Saturday? Did Nigeria, perhaps, have espionage agents in South Africa, or in the South African embassy in Washington? Olutunde was only a second secretary, the press attaché. He jotted down the number.

'Oh, and there was a call from a Carl Rosen. He says you know where to get him.'

'Right. Were all the kook calls the same?'

'They were different people, but they all concerned a statement you made on your radio program on Thursday about gays living lives of anxiety.'

He closed his eyes in semi-disbelief. The fact that the calls came together would mean that they were orchestrated.

'Leave the slips in my mail box,' Muir said. 'I'll play some Johnny Mathis for them next week.'

'Okay.' There was a hint of a chuckle in the woman's voice.

He called Olutunde.

'I'm sorry to call you on a Saturday, and to give you such short notice,' the Nigerian said in Oxbridge tones, 'but the editor of the Lagos *Daily Times* is coming in on Monday, and I'm giving a little press dinner for him that night. Can you come?'

'Dinners are difficult for me, during the week,' Muir said. 'I have an evening radio program. Sorry, though.'

'I understand.'

Muir called Carl.

'Maestro, art thou laboring at the opus?' Carl inquired. He sounded like a man who was looking forward to editing the Book-of-the-Month Club Number One selection.

'You're worried about the deadline.'

'*Exactement*, as they say.'

'So am I. I know you want me to give you the first twelve chapters without the last, but it's difficult to ignore the fact that we may have an arrest which may open up all sorts of new factors about Liversedge, and that we're almost certainly going to be overtaken by a trial.

The Liversedge story isn't going to go away — would a few weeks make much difference? I mean, I can't ignore — '

'Ignore, ignore, nonetheless. We've got a bestseller, so perfection isn't necessary. Just do us a Venus de Milo. We can always stick the arms on later.'

Muir thought: Am I really being unreasonable? I wish I had written a book before. How do you fashion a book to fit a breaking story that isn't over?

'I'll try,' he said.

'The difficult you must do at once,' Carl said, rephrasing someone — General Montgomery? 'The impossible takes a little longer.'

'I believe you,' Muir said.

★   ★   ★

He retrieved the typescript of the book from a drawer and put it on the desk. But moments later, the phone rang again. It was Remington.

'I'm doing a foreign-reaction piece to curtain-raise next week's arrivals for the funeral,' Remington said. 'You remember

181

Van Lo, the guy whom Livingstone negotiated with for the restoration of relations with Vietnam?'

'Yes.'

'They spent a month together in Geneva, and I thought he might have some sympathetic insights. He retired last year. But I see from the clips which Lola, here, has put together that you did an interview with him in 1977, in Ho Chi Minh City, and I wondered if you might have his home telephone number.'

'Let me look.'

Muir opened a drawer with his free hand and began sorting through a rumpled pile of old notepads and address books.

'How's the book going?' Remington asked.

'Like a Maserati, since Thursday night. From zero to sixty miles an hour in under six.'

'I believe you. Shame about Liversedge, though. Nice guy.'

Muir was twisting a finger around an old plastic book with multiple stains, buried under other books.

'How are your plans for the Senate?'

'Between you and I, I'm having some difficulty raising campaign funds. But I'll have to make my mind up soon, because my contract with the network is due for renewal in three months.'

'Have them write in free campaign time in the new contract.'

'Are you out of your mind?'

'Here it is,' said Muir. 'Van Lo. Forty-eight, ninety-nine, sixty-two.'

'Thanks.'

'Good luck. It's a Soviet communications satellite out there, and it's never functioned properly.'

'Imperialist slander,' said Reminington, 'I hope.'

It was only after Remington had put the receiver down that Muir remembered that Van Lo didn't speak English.

5

Muir had smuggled Vuissane into the Rotunda for the press viewing by hanging two of his cameras and one of his press cards around her neck. With her jeans, her absence of makeup and her long, rather unkempt hair, she looked, he thought, rather like some of the photographers he knew. They saw Gentiluomo leaving, with his entourage, as they came in. Adelaide was part of the President's group. She stopped for a moment to talk to Muir, who introduced her to Vuissane.

'She's bearing up marvelously well,' Vuissane said in admiration, after Adelaide had left. 'In a situation like that, I would disintegrate.'

'So would I,' Muir said sympathetically.

'The devil you would,' said Vuissane. 'You'd be making jokes about gravediggers and asking Gentiluomo if he thought the Mafia did it to put him into power.'

Muir half-smiled, looking away at the

two biers. Henry Roberts looked heavy and dominant, even on his back, even in death. He wore a dark gray suit. Only Roger's head showed from a sheet on the bier next door: His body had been badly broken in the blast, and Muir could see where the embalmer had repaired gashes on his face. But he looked reasonably serene, as though he had never known what hit him. The fact that he only got to show his head, while Roberts was visible down to his patent shoes, looked oddly vice-presidential.

Muir barely glanced at Roberts. He looked at Roger and thought of him at school and coming home from Korea and talking beside his fireplace in Providence and sitting in near-glory at the Vice President's residence a few days before, chuckling at one of his own anecdotes about a meeting he had once had with a religious leader in Iran. Muir felt his eyes moist. He looked around for Vuissane. She was squeezing off a few frames of Roberts, to justify her role. She looked up and their eyes met; she was red-eyed too.

Someone was asking her how much

longer she needed that position. It was a young girl assistant from Remington's network. Muir saw Remington's White House colleague, Adam Muziak, directing the crew. Then, Muziak stationed himself in front of the red rope, with the two biers and the Marines behind, and began to speak.

'Two statesmen have come to rest,' he began, heavily.

'Let's go,' said Vuissane.

'Okay.'

But Brad Williams emerged from one of the corridors at that moment, and Muir stopped. Williams kept him in conversation for nearly ten minutes. By then, the public had begun to enter, a long, shuffling, becalmed multitude. Even to Muir's sardonic mind, it was oddly moving, the way a theatrical adversity could briefly turn disparate people into a nation, for a moment. Those at the front of the line, who had waited longest, were mostly poor, or suburban, or provincial; but after about ten yards of this assembly line of grief had passed, there came the first custom-made suits and the more suitable-for-the-occasion dark dresses of their wives. As Muir and Vuissane became part of a single-file exodus down a corridor, he heard 'Psst!'

He looked around. A young black man in the entering line was trying to get his attention. Muir walked back; probably a radio fan, he thought.

'Mr. Muir? I thought if I come early I might catch you when the Press left. I need to talk to you.' Others were edging past him and looking at the two men talking. The young man's voice dropped. 'It's about the guy who kill Roger Liversedge. I see him.' Muir almost said: So did I. But the young man was saying: 'I follow him, afterward.'

'We can't talk here,' said Muir.

'You right. Look — I wanna see the body. I admired Mr. Liversedge. But I wanna see you later.'

Muir said: 'I'll be at Rufus' tonight. You know it?'

'Of course.'

'My friend is singing there, at eleven. Come about then, and we can talk after she leaves the table to go and sing.'

'Roger, man.' He walked off into the line.

'Who was that?' Vuissane asked when he rejoined her.

'Some late-music buff,' said Muir. 'He says he wants to catch your show.'

★   ★   ★

Vuissane and Muir ate at Vuissane's apartment. He drank Campari afterward and she drank milk. She never drank alcohol before singing, although she would drink afterward, when the show was over, to absorb the tension.

It was almost dark by the time they left for Rufus'. Coming up Twenty-ninth on to M, they noticed a crowd across the street, outside the Charing Cross. There were three patrol cars by the curb, their dome lights flashing. Parked around the corner on Thirtieth was a small blue-and-white paddy wagon. When they reached the group, Vuissane hung back but Muir pushed on through, showing one of his press cards aggressively.

At the door, a stocky police sergeant

stood in profile, his right arm stretched out like a frontier post and resting on the opposite lintel. Muir showed his card again.

'What's going on, sergeant?'

The sergeant looked inside without replying, and Muir followed his gaze. The bar was empty, but he could hear raised voices in the restaurant area. 'You've gotta be crazy,' an agitated man's voice was saying, apparently to the police.

A stentorian but calmer voice was saying: 'We just want you to come along with us and answer some questions. Now, drop that gun before somebody gets hurt.'

'You drop yours first,' said the other voice.

Was it a drug bust? There was something about the accent of the first voice, Muir decided. It was almost English. Was it Australian? Then he knew where he had heard a similar accent before, recently — on the Arena Stage Theatre. It was South African. He stiffened, remembering the conversation with Raines that afternoon. He looked away from the sergeant and saw a young blond patrolman with an almost pubertial blond mustache. He looked like the greenest man on the squad. The young patrolman was holding back onlookers; walking toward him, Muir smiled paternally, flashing his press card briefly and moving his mouth to the patrolman's ear. In these situations, normally a policeman would turn to face you head on, and ask 'Sir?' But the young patrolman was intimidated by Muir's avuncular manner, and bent an ear to catch Muir's words.

'This connected with the assassination?'

'Can't say, sir.' He sounded genuinely sorry not to be more helpful. Muir suspected that if the presence of all this force had nothing to do with the murder of the President, the patrolman would have said so, even if he had not been allowed to say what they *were* doing.

He looked around for Vuissane and saw her face at the back of the crowd. He raised a hand and smiled. She gestured back. Muir returned to the tavern door. The sergeant was still standing there like a tree with a branch across the path.

'Could I have a word with your lieutenant?'

'Does he know you?'

'Maybe.'

'You do the crime beat?'

'No.'

'This case is a little special,' the sergeant said. For the first time, he looked into Muir's eyes, and he no longer seemed officious.

'Press,' said a voice behind Muir's shoulder. He looked around, to find a thin man whom he didn't know.

'I just told your colleague, you'll have to wait a moment,' the sergeant snapped, on his guard again.

The new reporter turned to Muir.

'Mark Isaacs, Baltimore *Sun*.'

'Don Muir.'

'You hear the intercom traffic?'

'No.' If Isaacs had been monitoring police radio, Muir thought, he presumably belonged here, on the crime beat.

'It was sort of intentionally unclear. The code-figure was for murder, but the call for special handling suggested that it might be the assassination.'

Isaacs was talking in a low voice, looking away from the sergeant.

'Someone inside is shouting with a South African accent,' Muir said. 'He seems to be holed up, with a gun, holding the cops at bay.'

A black Buick arrived and parked behind the police cars, blocking a fire plug. Muir saw Jack Raines get out. That seemed confirmation enough.

'Smells like the feds,' said Isaacs.

'Let me talk to this fellow alone. I'll fill you in,' said Muir. He pushed his way through the gawkers and met Raines pushing his way in the opposite direction.

'Got a minute?'

'Just one.' Raines put an arm on Muir's shoulder and edged back toward the curb.

'Have you got the guy who did it?'

'Don, we're walking on eggshells here. The man in there claims diplomatic immunity.'

Muir kept his face impassive, conscious of watchers. 'But he's armed. In public. That's reason enough to — '

'He's also drunk. He says he had

— uh — ' Raines' voice dropped to a semi-whisper — 'Liversedge killed. The bartender didn't know whether to take him seriously or not, but he called the police.'

'What's his name? Was this the guy you said that you were looking for?'

Raines hesitated.

'I've interviewed some of them — South African diplomats, I mean — for a lobby story two years ago,' Muir said.

'Beukes.'

'That sounds familiar. I'm almost sure that name *is* on the List.'

'I know he's on the List,' said Raines, impatiently. 'But we know this person. And how many diplomats pack a magnum for a Saturday evening in Georgetown? I've gotta go.'

Muir tried to think of something to hold him back. 'There was something in the *Sun* about your investigating Puerto Ricans. You mentioned them this morning. The *Sun* said something about an arms cache.'

'We're checking it out.'

There was the sound of a gunshot from

within the tavern. No cry followed. Presumably the clients had all been evacuated and were already a part of the growing crowd of khibbitzers. Raines shouldered his way through them like a football player, dangling his simuli-leather FBI cardcase from slim fingers when he reached the door.

Muir rejoined Isaacs. Isaacs said: 'You see that man over there, the one in jeans who looks like Ernest Borgnine with a blue-rinse Kennedy wig?'

'What about him?'

'D'you know who he is?'

'I think he really is Borgnine in a wig,' Muir quipped.

'He's from Drug Enforcement. He handles internationals.'

'Then I think he's just another Georgetown spectator,' said Muir. 'The fed who just went in is on the assassination.' That was saying enough, he thought; he regretted having promised to fill Isaacs in on his brief talk with Raines at all. Was the full story about to break?

There was the sound of another shot, then three more shots in rapid succession.

Spectators at the front of the crowd tried to edge back, their arms stretched out, their buttocks against unseen bellies. At the door, the sergeant barked to the blond policeman: 'Johnson! Tell Cardozo to call in an ambulance!' The young policeman talked to a policewoman in one of the cruisers. The crowd fell back voluntarily as he went back and forth. Isaacs started walking back to the door, and Muir followed him. They looked over the sergeant's arm again. Just inside the archway to the restaurant area they could see two policemen, one with his back turned toward them, both with drawn pistols. One, in profile, was a stocky man of thirty or so, with a black mustache. He was looking anxiously at shoes on the floor: The shoes obviously had feet in them, but they weren't moving, and the legs and the rest of the body were out of sight. The shoes were black and solid and plain. They appeared to be policemen's shoes.

A minute later, the ambulance arrived, its siren wailing impending doom. Two men jumped out of the cabin and hurried around to the back, opening up the rear doors and pulling out two stretchers. There was another shot, the sounds of a scuffle involving furniture, and a cry. The crowd had now moved back a solid three yards, and the ambulance crew were able to rush the folded stretchers across the sidewalk and into the Charing Cross without impediment. Isaacs, followed by Muir, tried to go in with them, but the sergeant stopped them. Muir gave up on the entry bid and walked back to the crowd, giving a nod to Vuissane. He heard Isaacs arguing, shouting the word 'Press', and the sergeant saying, irritably: 'You people cause all the trouble.' When Isaacs rejoined him, Muir said: 'I hear the sergeant thinks we caused the assassination.'

Isaacs lit a cigarette. 'I think he's right,' he said, pokerfaced. He drew on the cigarette again. 'I think the Washington press killed Liversedge. He was there, a quarter of a mile from the South Lawn, and he got to thinking of all those press conferences that loomed ahead, the newspaper cartoons, and he just blew the plane up.'

'Good a theory as any,' said Muir.

Vuissane had joined them and was listening.

Isaacs went on: 'I think he felt like one of those North Korean infiltrators who are about to be captured, and he didn't want to be captured by the Washington press, so he did like the North Koreans: He just pulled a pin on a grenade and held it against his head.'

'It's just as well they always keep a stock of grenades in that helicopter for presidents to play with,' said Muir.

Vuissane was staring at their banter in disbelief.

'I'm surprised, though,' Isaacs said, 'since he'd survived the vice presidency. John Nance Garner said the vice presidency wasn't worth a vase of hot spit.'

'I know,' said Muir, 'I wrote the book, or I'm in the process of doing so.'

The stretcher bearers reappeared. There were now four of them, two of them police. The policeman lying on the first stretcher could have been unconscious, but there was no plasma bottle and there was an aura about the bearers which said that he was dead. Behind came two policemen carrying a man strapped down to another stretcher. The man was fair and stocky and had a heavy bruise above one eye, as though he had gone down fighting. He wasn't the Thompson's Boatyard figure Muir had seen: If Raines had really cracked the case, there must be at least two people involved.

'You're crazy,' the man on the stretcher was still saying. The voice sounded slurred.

Vuissane looked away. 'I want to go home,' she said.

Muir said: 'You want to skip the show? You want to call Rufus', or shall I go along and explain?'

'No, I mean I want to go back to France,' Vuissane said. 'Mr. Roberts, Mr. Liversedge, now this. There is too much violence in this country.'

'That's how the West was won. It's the American way,' said Muir. 'By the way, this is Mark Isaacs,' he said in English.

'Mark, this is Vuissane.'

'I've heard you sing,' Isaacs said.

Vuissane wasn't listening and continued in French, ignoring Isaacs. 'How can you go on like this, so soon after Roger's death?'

'I didn't mean to sound cynical,' said Muir. That sounded terribly bland. He added: 'Only slightly cynical.'

'I've got to go,' said Isaacs. 'Gotta follow that ambulance.'

Raines came out. Muir turned to speak to him, but Raines said quickly: 'Call me tomorrow morning.'

★　★　★

They reached Rufus' just before ten. In the half light, as they were shown to a table near the raised area where the piano stood, Muir saw the usual mixture of Georgetown faces and tourists, businessmen with young women, well-heeled students with younger women, Hill aides, people in the Roberts administration who might soon be leaving town, here and there some homosexual couples. An

199

elderly black pianist was playing background, drinkers' music. A waitress took their orders. He began to drink beer. Vuissane drank orange juice. For many minutes, they said almost nothing. He knew that she was thinking of the Rotunda scene, the shoot-out at the Charing Cross. He was thinking of the young black man, and what might be just another false trail. He had difficulty convincing himself that Beukes had been behind the assassination; anything like that could only rebound against his government, now beleaguered by revolution. But then again, he *had* shot a policeman just now: Even in drunkenness, and probably misguidedly claiming self-defense, that was pretty wild, for a diplomat. Only after the second beer, on top of the Camparis and the excitement on the sidewalk, did Muir begin to unwind. Now, he tried hard to ensure that his conversation would sound less callously cynical, and Vuissane seemed to relax a little.

He found himself watching her, and sharing the effort she was making to rid herself of the tension that always preceded a performance, and that was clearly worse just now, for a multitude of obvious reasons. He needed, he knew, to think less about the goddam bestseller he was birthing in an atmosphere of hope, frustration, confusion and cynicism, mixed with the frequent consciousness of remorse that he was profiting from Roger's death. He needed to think more about her, even though her problems seemed at times, to him, to be less than his. She was not, he reminded himself, in her own environment. His principal problem, he reflected, was that he was.

At five minutes before eleven, she went to the bathroom. When he saw her again, she was walking on, with her guitar, and the pianist who had been playing until then began introducing her.

Vuissane blew Muir a kiss, then set her gaze on the audience.

'Good evening. I have a friend who likes 'Solitaire',' Vuissane said. 'He doesn't know it, but I have written French words so I can sing it in my own way, without sounding funny.'

She struck a chord. He was moved. Listening, he knew he loved Vuissane despite his extraordinary indulgence of that afternoon. Her voice rolled over him; the guitar seemed to be a part of her as well. He was cut off for a moment from everything and everyone else around. But before she could finish, he felt a rough touch on his arm. He looked up and saw the young black man who had talked to him in the Rotunda, and who had arranged to meet him there at that time.

'Wilfred,' the man said. 'Wilfred Jacks.'

'Sit down. Have a drink.'

'Whiskey. On the rocks.'

Muir listened to the end of Vuissane's song, and applauded. She was smiling at him broadly. The audience had apparently liked it too, and was showing its approval. Next, she sang an old French ballad. He closed his mind to French, and turned to Jacks: 'So. Tell me what you saw.'

Jacks was dark, with rough, dignified African features which were transformed and debased by an American expression as he began to speak. Working class, Muir thought; not very educated, but smart

— or at least assertive.

'Well, I was in the grass at Thompson's Boatyard with this chick. We met at Paul's Mall, the disco, and she was high, and well, anyway, she's sleepin' it off after we done our thing, and I'm lookin' 'round at the stars, and then I hear the helo comin' in. I was high too, and for a moment I thought I was back in Nam.'

The bourbon came and he took a big gulp. Jacks looked about thirty, but Muir knew from his Vietnam experience that he must be about ten years older.

'Well, I see the explosion. I didn't know President Roberts died, or who's in the chopper. And then I see this dude runnin' from the parkin' lot. I belt up my pants and took off after him.'

'I live at the Watergate. I was standing on my terrace and I saw the figure running away, but I never saw you.'

'I was huggin' the bushes, like in Nam. I don' wan' him to see me. He run under the freeway. I stay in the shadows and follow him, through the little tunnel. I see him go up Twenty-ninth. I'm about half a block back.

'At M, this guy slow to a walk and turn left. When I get to the corner, he gettin' into a cab. I just see his butt, I never see his face. I stop another cab. I was lucky they was so close. An' I say: 'Follow that cab.' The driver thought I was jivin' him but I tell him 'Don' talk, man, drive!' Well, he catch up with the other cab at Washington Circle. Then we get split up in the traffic around the Circle. We follow it down Pennsylvania Avenue. We hit a red light after the other cab get through. I guess that's about Eighteenth. Yeah, Eighteenth. Finally, the other cab stop on Pennsylvania Avenue, just before Seventeenth. We a block away, on the red light. It's a long block. I pay my man off at that light and begin runnin'. The guy's gone down Seventeenth, of that I'm positive. I never did find him again.'

'There are George Washington University residential buildings not far from there,' Muir said.

'And a funny old hotel behind.'

'I wonder why he didn't take the cab all the way to where he was going.'

'Maybe he know I'm following him. Maybe he jus' didn' wan' the hackie to know where he was going.'

'He was short. What else? You're really sure it was a man?'

'Oh, I think so, yeah. He didn't have no curves.'

'There are women like that.'

'He didn't run like a woman.'

'A woman only runs in the way you mean because of her figure. Some women can be rather masculine.'

'Yeah. Maybe.'

Vuissane's voice crescended and stopped. She plonked a final bar. There was applause again. Muir looked up and applauded too, catching her eye. She was peering against the light at Jacks.

'I didn't hear you,' Muir said, as the applause receded.

'I'm sayin' he had short hair, not quite a military cut but almost.'

Muir thought: Maybe he was going into the Old Executive Office Building. Was Liversedge murdered by some agency of the Government? He began to bite the inside of his lip with something that felt like fear. Vuissane's voice and guitar had begun to take over the room again. He leaned toward Jacks' ear.

'Why didn't you go to the police?'

'Me? Man! I'm in violation of parole. I'm not suppose' to leave Bismarck, North Dakota. But I know you knew Mr. Liversedge, that you writin' a book about him, an' I figure you'd wanna find the motherfucker who wasted him.'

'I do. And I thank you. Is there anywhere I can contact you?'

Jacks pulled a piece off a matchbook and wrote down a number. Muir didn't recognize the first three digits: It must be somewhere in Northeast, he thought.

'That's my steady woman, her number. Louise. Say you want to leave a message for me. Tell me to call you, or whatever.'

Muir slipped the piece of card into his wallet; then, he had a second thought. 'Here, I can give you my number,' he said. But Jacks was already on his way to the door. Muir reflected that he didn't know if the number he had been given was actually Louise's, or whether there was really a Louise in Jacks' life. But he tended to believe the part about violating parole. Oh well, his own number was in the book.

6

When they got back to Muir's apartment at two a.m., Vuissane was too tired, too melancholy because of the Rotunda experience and the shoot-out, to want to make love. Muir was glad. Mrs. No-Name was no doubt servicing her complaisant husband, and not only with her cuisine, but Muir felt drained. He thought: No wonder her husband goes along with her adventures; it would be nice to have a free supply of Campari, but to be obliged to drink a gallon of the stuff every day — you'd have to share.

Although both of them were tired, neither of them felt sleepy. His nerves were taut, and he could see and sense from the half-frown on her face that hers were, too. Vuissane was lying beside him in the moonlit room, still talking about the scene in the Rotunda, and he was thinking both about Raines and about Jacks' story. He had told Vuissane once again that Jacks was a fan of her show.

'You seemed to find him interesting,' Vuissane had said, probing.

'He knew a hell of a lot about Oscar Peterson,' Muir had murmured.

Now, she was talking about Henry Roberts.

'You're lucky the Press never found out that you were teaching him how to pronounce French that night,' Muir said. 'They'd have been all over you for interviews. About how he was, what he was saying. Maybe I should have interviewed you myself. You practically heard his last words.'

'Yes, I did,' she said.

'I'm surprised no-one got your name from the White House roster.'

'I don't remember anyone putting me on a roster.'

'You weren't signed in? Strange.'

Vuissane got up, quickly and with an air of impatience; she went to the kitchen for a beer. When she returned, she said: 'What did you think about President Roberts, really?'

'He was okay,' Muir said guardedly. 'A

sharp pol. Moderate. Not very bright, but how many presidents are? You remember the stories they used to tell about Eisenhower? I guess you don't. There was one where Mamie comes in from town and finds him sitting on the edge of the bed with a gun to his head. 'Oh Ike,' she says, 'don't fool around' — 'Don't laugh,' he says, 'you're next!' '

He was trying to relax her, but perhaps he was only succeeding in sounding cynical again. He thought of Isaacs' prankish theory about Liversedge blowing himself up to avoid the press.

'There was a similar joke about Gerry Ford. The question was: What do you do if Gerry Ford enters a room with a pin in his hand? And the answer was: You run, because it means he has a grenade in his mouth.'

'Did you support Roberts' election?' Vuissane asked.

'I guess if voting were compulsory in this country, as it is in some, I'd have voted for him. But for a political reporter to vote is rather like a monk judging a beauty contest.'

'I liked President Roberts. I felt sorry for him. I suppose you are more concerned about Mr. Liversedge.'

She had difficulty calling Roger, Roger. Sometimes she forced herself to do it; but in France, you didn't call a Vice President of the Republic by his first name.

'So is the rest of the Press, which is perhaps why they never got on to you about seeing Roberts on his last night.'

'Mr. Liversedge was very kind to me,' Vuissane said, looking at the ceiling. 'When you suggested it that time, he had me over to sing, following the dinner for the Belgian prime minister. And he talked to me afterward, when the Belgians and all the other guests had left, and he was very *sympathique*.'

So *Monsieur Liversedge* too had been *sympathique*. 'You never told me,' Muir said. 'What did he say?'

'Oh, he told me about you at high school, and how you wrote a letter to the principal on the Sheriff's notepaper and signed the Sheriff's name and the poor *bonhomme* thought he was in trouble.'

'Fancy him remembering that.'

'And about some of the things you both did at college. And he talked about Korea. It was the only foreign experience of his life until he became Vice President.'

'Did he talk about Janet, his Korean girlfriend?'

'Yes, he was very wistful about Janet.'

'I never quite found out, in talking to him, why he never married Janet.'

'He couldn't.'

'I thought of that. He was fresh out of college, but he was already ambitious. I guess, in those days, it would still have hurt his political career if he'd married anyone who wasn't the right shade, and a foreigner. But Koreans were a minority too. I'm not sure it would have mattered. In any event, I never met Janet — I was still at Brown.'

'He talked about Mitsuko, the Japanese woman in Providence, too. He couldn't marry her, either.'

'Oh, by then, in the 'Sixties, I don't think it would have mattered. He never gave me that as a reason. He was evasive.'

'You don't understand, Donald. He told me something in private which I suppose I can tell you now. You may need it for the book. He was impotent.'

Muir let the words sink in. The very adjective seemed somehow to have less finality in French: *Impuissant* literally meant powerless, which everyone was in one way or another. He thought: How could you know someone for forty-seven years and not know that?

'Truly?'

He thought: That could explain some things about Roger that no-one, including myself, had ever been clear about.

'A lot of men in politics are like that,' Vuissane said, matter-of-factly and tolerantly. 'They compensate for one power they lack by spending all their time on power itself. You didn't know?'

'It's an interesting thought.'

'There was Boumedienne in Algeria, and Ben Bella before him. And Qaddafi in Libya. There was Shaka, the king of the Zulus, a hundred years ago. Maybe Hitler.'

'Arafat? I mean, you never hear anything.'

'Possibly. And there was that British

213

prime minister in the 'Seventies, what was his name?'

'Roger did seem to enjoy the sexual life of others more than his own. Was he a *voyeur*?'

'Of a sort, I suppose,' Vuissane said. 'He talked a lot that night. He was a sort of matchmaker for other men.'

'That's one way of describing it.'

He slipped out of bed in his turn and went to the refrigerator for another beer. When he returned, he was thinking again of Thursday night. 'How about Roberts?' he asked. 'How did you get to sing at the White House? Was it what the *Post* and the *Sun* said about your singing, at Roger's Belgian evening?'

'I think Mr. Liversedge told the President about me and the President apparently said he wanted to see me, and that the only way was to invite me to sing at that *soirée* for the Cambodians, who understand French.'

'He wanted to *see* you?'

'He was a lonely man. All that power and responsibility. You know what his wife is like.'

'What are you saying?'

'He said at the end of the *soirée* that he would arrange for me to visit the White House privately — '

'After he's seen you, on Roger's recommendation,' Muir said, thinking aloud.

'Yes. And so I went there, Thursday night.'

'And they didn't put you on the roster.'

'I don't think so.' She sipped beer. 'There was something I didn't tell you. It wasn't a woman in the President's office who called me. It was Mr. Liversedge, from Camp David. He said the President was coming back from Camp David, and so on, that I should go to the White House to help him with the French speech. It was all, sort of, private. I wasn't supposed to tell anyone.'

Muir raised his head from the pillow. 'Which entrance did you use?'

'The front.'

'The north portico?'

'What's a *portique*? The driveway, yes. Where the dignitaries come. Mr. Wong was waiting for me and he took me to the private quarters, the library.'

'How did the hour go?'

'We went over his speech, and I wrote in some pronunciation he would understand. His accent was awful. I don't think he ever did French at high school. I suggested some changes that made the speech easier for him to read. He told me to mark them in red, so that the State Department could look at them.'

'Pity. You could have made him say something outrageous.' But then, of course, he thought, Roberts never got to make that speech. 'Did he have another appointment at eight?'

'No, we just went on, and then he invited me to eat.'

'You were pretty informally attired to face the White House crystal.'

'Oh, we just ate in the library. He sent for Mr. Wong and said he wanted a club sandwich. He said: 'Would you like a club sandwich, too?' I didn't want to tell him that I didn't like club sandwiches, so I said yes.'

'That sounds like Roberts. Not much

finesse, especially since he became president. When did you leave him?'

'Later. We talked a long time.'

'What did he talk about?'

'All sorts of things. Nothing profound.'

'Were you the last person to see him alive, d'you think?'

'Yes.'

'What were his last words, d'you remember?'

' 'Ring the bell'.'

She was leaning away from him now. There was a touch of aggressiveness in her voice, as though she had resented his question.

'So Mr. Wong came.'

'Yes.'

'What for?'

'To help the President.'

'Help him?'

She swung round and said: 'Why are you asking me? No-one could help him any more. He was dead!'

'He died in the library?'

She said nothing for a moment. Then: 'You heard the announcement. No-one ever said that he died in the library. The announcement said he died in bed.'

'You were in his bedroom, Vuissane?'

'No. Mr. Wong put him to bed.'

'Why?'

'Because it would not have seemed correct that he die in the library.'

'Seemed? But you said he died in bed.'

'I said that was what the White House said, and the papers said.' She paused. 'Donald, he was a lonely man. He needed — oh, to relax. And he had promised me my labor permit, and more concerts at the White House.'

'I bet.' He thought of Mrs. No-Name. He wondered whether Roberts had opted for the missionary position or whether Vuissane had straddled him. Now, what had seemed like over-reaction on Vuissane's part, on the morning after Roberts' death, finally made sense. Visiting the Rotunda must have been even more of an ordeal for her than he had thought.

'Mr. Wong had to put the — the — ' she avoided the word corpse — 'the President in his pajamas and put him to bed.'

'How did that little guy manage to lift Roberts?'

'Well, he had to undress him first. Did you think he was undressed?' Her concern for the President's dignity now seemed a little comic.

'You mean you were giving him the Japanese telephone?' It was the idiomatic French phrase for fellatio.

She obviously resented the humor in his voice. 'After all, *mon ami*, he was the President,' she said seriously. 'I was rendering a service.'

Muir wondered if the rising indignation that his humor masked was hypocritical, after all. If Vuissane had been one of Roberts' secretaries and had had to put up with his coarse temper, would he have felt less indignant against the President?

He said: 'It reminds me of Félix Faure?'

'The President of France?'

'Yes. He died of a heart attack in a Paris bordello in 1899. They had to carry him back to the Elysée to 'die' again.'

'I didn't know he died that way.'

'You weren't paying attention in history class.'

'The nuns would never have taught us that. What happened to the girl?'

'They should have given her a pension and the Legion of Honor to keep her mouth shut. But they probably goofed, because everybody knew the story. I'm sure she lived well, to the end of her career, as the woman who screwed the Chief of State to mortality.'

In the moonlight, he saw her pout. He knew that she was about to say that he was 'disgusting'. It was an adjective she used at least once a day. Instead, she said: 'You know, you'd never be able to sing ballads.'

'I love the fact that you do,' he said.

She moved over, and rested her head in the crook of his shoulder.

'How did Hwan get him to bed?' he asked.

'He dragged him. He's very strong for his size, wiry. He was in the Army for many years, remember? I guess he keeps fit. But he had to go around to the other side of the bed and lean over and pull the

President across by his hands, then straighten him up and put the sheet over him. He left him with one hand out toward the bell-push. I watched him from the door.'

'You didn't help him?'

'I just couldn't.'

'No — uh — tell-tale signs?'

'Mr. Wong wiped him off.'

'Did Hwan see you out?'

'Yes. Then he went back to call a doctor.'

Muir imagined the scene. 'So the President died with a smile on his face?'

Finally, Vuissane said it: 'You are disgusting.' Muir felt better: There was humor, now, in both their voices.

She fell asleep soon, apparently relieved to have unburdened herself. In the moonlight reflected from the river, he looked at her mouth against his shoulder, the mouth that had sung into his heart and into the minds of others, the mouth that had unintentionally dispatched the fortieth President to the bosom of Abraham and probably caused the assassination of Roger Liversedge and made a small-time Hartford honcho into the new chief executive of the United States. And saved Muir's book.

* * *

In his dream, he was sitting on a park bench in Newport with Roger Liversedge. People were walking by, taking no notice of the Governor. Liversedge was saying: 'I wish you hadn't talked to those FBI goons about what I did for Governor Irwin, and my sexy stories.'

Muir said: 'But you're dead now, Roger. It can't hurt. It might help them find your killer.'

'But it will look bad on the legislative calendar,' Liversedge retorted, absurdly. 'It wouldn't have mattered if the loan to the tomato-growers had gone through. But now, as you know, I've bought a Peugeot.'

A subservient man in rags, a sort of waterfront bum, approached and said to Liversedge: 'There's a call for you, sir. You can take it in the park privy.' Muir heard the phone.

Liversedge got up impatiently. There was something else that Muir wanted to say to him, but it was too late, for he was already awake, and his own phone was ringing. He dragged himself from the bed.

'Muir,' he said sleepily into the receiver.

'Solly. Missa Muir, you sleeping, no?'

'That's all right, Hwan. You wanted to come over, today.'

'Prease. Not wanna disturb you. But yes, rater.'

Before Vuissane and Muir had gone to bed earlier that morning, a message left with the desk downstairs had said that there would be a State Department briefing that day, at twelve, about a South African diplomat who had been arrested, possibly in connection with the Liversedge assassination.

'Would you like to come at two?'

'Oh. Yes, Missa Muir. At two.'

'See you.'

'Yes. Tank you. Okay.'

★ ★ ★

The reporters in the State Department briefing room were dressed for Sunday — open-necked shirts, even some tennis shorts. Only the TV people wore ties.

Watson, the State Department spokesman, announced that Johannes Beukes, a member of the South African embassy, had been arrested the night before, after shots were exchanged in a Georgetown restaurant. A policeman had been killed, and Beukes had been injured. Beukes had been under investigation for some time, in connection with the mysterious deaths of some black South African students and others, thought to be members of a revolutionary organization. The investigation had been hampered by Beukes' diplomatic immunity. A cache of arms had been discovered at Beukes' residence.

An agency correspondent asked: 'Is Beukes suspected of being President Liversedge's assassin? Is that what you're saying?'

The spokesman said: 'The FBI is apparently investigating the possibility of a hit team.'

'You mean Beukes was their 'control'?'

'A connection is being investigated.'

'What's an arms cache?' asked a booming voice. Muir recognized the tones of Nestor Nieberling, an extreme rightwing columnist who regularly defended the South African government. 'Surely South African diplomats are entitled to have guns in their homes to defend themselves? What news do you have on the Puerto Rican arms cache found yesterday?'

Muir found his mind drifting, as it often did when Nieberling was asking his tendentious questions. Watson was saying: 'Puerto Rico is part of the United States. The State Department has nothing to report on Puerto Rico.' He was looking at Muir, whose arm was half-raised.

'Did the South African cache contain any shoulder-fired missile-launchers?' Muir asked.

'I can't answer that.'

Nieberling was booming again. 'That's crucial! If they found only protective side-arms — '

Watson was ignoring him. 'Yes?' he said, pointing to Remington. Muir went full volume into his microphone: 'May I put that question another way?'

'Go ahead, Don.'

Muir was thinking that South Africa didn't manufacture any shoulder-fired missiles of its own. He said: 'Can I ask you this? Did they find any weapons that were not of South African manufacture?'

'Good try, Don,' said Watson, pointing determinedly now at Remington. Nieberling's rightwing tones were shouting stridently: 'Answer Muir's question!' and Remington was saying: 'Has the embassy been asked to waive Beukes' immunity?'

Watson devised an evasive answer which left the question hanging. Muir had the feeling that they were all wasting time. Watson's job was to answer questions, but not to answer questions, at times like this.

★　★　★

After Muir returned home, he called Raines, as Raines had asked him to do, but Raines was not in his office. He waited for Wong Hwan. The Taiwanese butler was on time. He sat on the same portion of the sofa that he had occupied before. Trim and polite, he was still a butler talking to the friend of 'Governor' Liversedge. He asked again what Muir had seen. Muir told him again about the explosion, the single rotary blade emerging from the water. Vuissane walked by, barefoot, coming out of the bedroom where she had been watching television. She said hello to Wong, and disappeared into the kitchen.

Wong suddenly changed the subject, as though still in shock from the two deaths and finding it hard to concentrate. Now he was talking about Taiwan, about what he saw as the chances for Taiwanese independence. It was Muir's turn to find it hard to concentrate.

'Have you had lunch, Mr. Wong?' Vuissane called from the kitchen. She sounded calm. It was hard to remember that she and Wong shared such a secret.

'Oh. Yes,' said Wong.

'Coffee? Iced tea?'

'Prease. Ice tea. Tank you.'

Muir said: 'Hwan, she has told me how

President Roberts died.'

'Oh. Learry? It would be teb'ble if ev'one knew.'

'It came out by accident,' Muir said. 'Neither of us will tell anyone.'

'Plezident Loberts velly good man. Would be teb'ble for countly, teb'ble for Mizz Loberts, the famiry. No use.'

'No, I agree, it would just be gossip,' Muir said. 'It would serve no useful purpose that people should know. People believe he died of a heart attack. He did. That's natural causes. Everyone knew he had a heart condition.'

'So grad.' Muir was scarcely noticing Wong's intense accent, his mispronunciations. He realized Wong meant that he was glad Muir saw things the same way he did.

'Only Gov'nor Riv'sedge would have told,' Wong said. 'He always told about tings like that. He told me many storlies. Sometimes I shock.'

'You have a point there,' said Muir. 'Here's your tea coming in.'

'Oh. Tank you.' He was half-rising, half-bowing toward Vuissane, who smiled and went back to the kitchen.

'I like Gov'nor Riv'sedge,' Wong said, 'but he — uh — indiscleet.'

'Well, we don't have to worry about that now.'

'Gov'nor Riv'sedge know about Miss Visson and the Plezident. He allange it.'

'Yes.'

'Would have tol' ev'one.'

'You may be right,' said Muir. He rose and walked to a side table, opened a can of tobacco, picked up a pipe and began filling it. 'We don't have to worry about that now,' he said again. 'A Redeye took care of that.'

'You tink a Ledeye?'

'I'd forgotten you were an old artillery hand. You think it was a Stinger?'

'No. Omblust.' That was what it sounded like. Muir paused in the act of lighting his pipe.

'Ah, Armbrust. The German weapon?'

'Tat one used by Taiwan fellah who attack Beijing embassy last year,' Wong said.

Muir remembered the incident. A Taiwanese nationalist had finally been found and sentenced to fifteen years. The Armbrust was a disposable, one-time affair. Was Wong saying that there were more around? With whom? The Taiwanese?

'It only had a short range,' Muir said.

'Yes, but enough,' said Wong. 'Veh liddle backfire, no damage be'ind.'

'Very little backfire?'

'Yes. About ten feet, under light conditions.'

'Under the right conditions,' Muir echoed.

Wong seemed remarkably knowledgeable, for a butler, even for one who had served in the artillery.

'You keep up with these things, I see.'

'I lead the books.'

'And you think it was an Armbrust that they found.'

'Sure.'

What did he mean — sure? Did he mean it literally, or was he just using the word to say 'That's right — that's what I think'? A scenario began to develop in Muir's mind. He saw again the slight, lithe running figure with the short hair, not unlike Mrs. No-Name's. He thought of Jacks following the man in a taxi, and the man getting off near Seventeenth Street — near the White House. Wong? Was that why he was so concerned to know exactly what Muir had seen? He could have gone in through the Old Executive Office Building and through the underground corridor to the West Wing and up to his apartment. He could move in and out without question. And certainly without suspicion. Who would ever think of Wong? It was clear he had Taiwanese nationalist sympathies: Did they cache their weapons with him? They couldn't find a safer and less likely place than the quarters of the White House butler. The Armbrust came in two pieces. You could probably have half a dozen, and the missiles to match, in a foot locker. He would only have needed one. And then Muir thought of the kitchen gloves the police had found: They must have come from Wong's White House kitchen.

Wong was saying again: 'You and Miss Visson will say nutting.' It was partly a question, partly a sort of reassurance.

Nothing about what? Muir thought.

'Only make scandal. No use,' Wong went on.

Muir wanted to tell Wong that he knew that he had killed Roger Liversedge to spare President Roberts' memory and the feelings of the family from the blabbermouth that the cool, patrician Rhode Islander with the secret problem of his own had always been about the sex stories of politicians. But he knew that he could not tell Wong that. Wong had not admitted anything. He had only explained a theory about a weapon. It was only Wong's inadequate English that made him unable to dissemble more skillfully. But if Muir said more, he might learn. And if he learned, this time it would certainly be — what was it again? — misprision of a felony. And what a felony!

Muir said only: 'I saw a man running away. A short man. Slim.'

'Is tat so?' said Wong.

'But I never got a good look at him,' Muir added. 'I never saw his face.'

'So.'

* * *

After Wong had left, Muir faced the enormity of the thought that he and Wong were presumably the only two people who knew who had assassinated the President of the United States. He also knew — another enormity — that he could never reveal it, because of Vuissane. The least it might do would be to sabotage her labor permit and get her expelled — the extinction of the mercenary reason why she had accommodated President Roberts in the first place. It was yet another weight that Muir could never share with Vuissane what he had discovered, either. He took down *Jane's Weapons Systems* from a bookshelf and looked up what Wong had called the Omblust. He was still reading the reference when he was interrupted by a phone call. It was Raines.

'Since you were on the street in Georgetown last night and saw the thing at the Charing Cross, I thought I'd better call and advise you on deep background not to go abundance on Beukes — you know what I mean?'

Muir was not a card player but he understood. 'You think it's another false trail?' he asked, trying hard to sound surprised.

'As you already know, we have things on him related to the deaths of African students and others — that was in the State Department briefing, you'll recall — and, also on DB, we do have an affidavit saying he boasted of having ordered Liversedge's death; but he was gassed to the gills at the time, and it looks as though it was just a South African's idea of a joke. On the record, you can say a source says that no decision has been made to charge Beukes in the Liversedge assassination or to bring him before a grand jury. Of course, the killing of the policeman is another matter, but he does have immunity.'

'Right.' Taking advantage of the cooperative air in their conversation, Muir went on: 'I understand that you've recovered the launcher of an Armbrust, and that it's manufactured by Messerschmitt-Bolkow-Blohm of Munich and has a range of three hundred meters and is normally used against tanks.' He was reading from *Jane's Weapons Systems*. He heard Raines suck in his breath slightly, either with displeasure or surprise to hear Muir identify the weapon. Muir guessed that if he asked Raines to confirm what he had just said, Raines would probably decline to do so; instead, he added quickly: 'Did you recover one Armbrust launcher or two?' The question was stupid on its face; everyone agreed that there had been only one explosion, and there could have been no possible reason for the assassin to make a second launch. But Raines took the bait.

'Only one,' he said, giving Muir the confirmation on the make of the weapon he wanted. Muir thought: It has to be Wong.

'That's on background, okay?' Raines asked.

'Of course. I also understand that the Armbrusts we have in this country are stored at White Sands.' He was making a reasonable guess, but deceiving Raines once more with the word 'understand'.

Raines was apparently still convinced that Muir had another source. He said: 'I believe we have about four hundred of them in the U.S. for evaluation — I don't guarantee the exactness of that figure — and that, yes, most of them are kept at White Sands Missile Range in New Mexico. You may recall that an Armbrust was used by that Taiwanese guy against the Chinese embassy.'

'Yes.'

'You'll remember that the one used then was one of four which had been stolen from the Army Proving Grounds at Aberdeen, Maryland, where they were being dismantled for analysis.'

This was a detail which Muir had forgotten, if indeed he had ever heard it, but he said: 'Oh, yeah.'

'I don't think we ever did account for the other three,' Raines said. He seemed to be thinking aloud when he added: 'Of course, there's a link between Taiwan and South Africa.'

Muir smiled at the non-sequitur. There were, he knew, trade links, some of them secret, between the governments of

Taiwan and South Africa, but certainly no links between Pretoria and the Taiwanese independentists, who were opposed to both the Chinese and Taiwanese governments.

'By the way, the tap — ' Muir began.

'Oh, I had the tap on your line removed yesterday,' Raines said. 'I should have mentioned — we'd hardly be having this conversation if I hadn't. I see that dame never called back.'

'Just some crazy broad, I guess,' said Muir. 'She probably really wanted a date.'

'You flatter yourself,' said Raines.

★   ★   ★

After Raines rang off, Muir spent the rest of the afternoon writing. He rewrote the start of the book, beginning with his eyewitness account of Roger's death. He put in the indistinguishable running figure. He quoted Jacks, without giving Jacks' name: He would discuss that with the publisher's lawyers later. He began to rewrite sections, taking into account that Roger had eventually become President and that he had died. Parts of the book that had previously seemed rather dull came to life now that Liversedge had been President and even more now that he had become a national martyr. His very blackness became more significant, as though it had marked him for such a fate — defeat in the hour of victory — from the start. And he began to rewrite the Korean chapter, in the light of the other great tragedy, the hidden one, of Liversedge's existence. He would have to talk to Mitsuko, in Providence, again.

Vuissane came out of the bedroom at one point to join him; but after a greeting, she decided not to disturb his writing. She returned to watch the tennis on television. From time to time, he looked up from his desk, at the sunshine on the river and the families out in skiffs. It seemed a very normal summer Sunday in Washington.

It was at about five that Vuissane reappeared in the living room, flushed.

'Come quickly. They're saying something on the television. A man has confessed to the assassination.'

Muir felt a hollow in his throat. If the whole purpose of Wong's action was to cover a secret, why would he talk? Had the internal pressures just been too great? Muir followed Vuissane to the bedroom. The tennis was still on, with the commentary and the plock of balls, but with words now appearing across the bottom of the screen. A man had contacted the Washington *Post* and confessed to the killing, the words said, as the commentator's voice rose with 'Another fantastic save from the back of the court by Rosario.' The printed words said that the man who had confessed to killing Liversedge had also announced that he was committing suicide, and his body had since been found. Muir stiffened, awaiting the rest. 'Not quite! Deuce!' said the commentator. The bulletin went on to say that the man's name was Leroy Flug, and he had shot himself in a motel in Leander, Alabama, which was his hometown. That was all, except for a burst of applause from Wimbledon as somebody called Rosario took the decisive set. The tennis commentary went on, the commentator in London unaware that he had been interrupted in any way, and recording the crowd's delight at the win by an unseeded player.

'It's solved. Already,' Vuissane said. In his mind, it sounded as though she were applauding too.

'Call me if there's more,' said Muir.

He went back to the book, but now he was distracted by this curious new development. At six, he watched the local-station news and also tuned to an all-news radio. The FBI had worked quickly, both reports agreed, and they had checked out the man's story. An FBI spokesman was on the TV screen, saying: 'Flug was convicted three times for violence against blacks. He was sentenced to six months for murdering a black man in Alabama in the Fifties, and to ten years for killing a black prostitute, a decade later, in Tennessee. He served just over six years in a Tennessee penitentiary. More recently, he was sentenced a year in Virginia, and served nine months, for assaulting a black policeman outside a Shirlington tavern. Flug wrote two threatening letters to the Vice President, one in 1981 and one the following year. He was investigated by the Secret Service and the FBI and agreed on both occasions to undergo psychiatric treatment. He was a virtually lifelong member of the Ku Klux Klan. Police in all states were looking for him, along with many other individuals of a similar type, after the assassination; but he was still being sought when he telephoned the Washington *Post* earlier today. He shot himself in a motel, apparently a few moments later.

'Our inquiries indicate that he had been renting a room in Georgetown for the past few weeks, not far from the scene of the assassination. He lived separated from his wife, who is in San Diego.'

A reporter came on, saying that the FBI spokesman had answered questions. Then, there was a cut of a reporter at the hastily-called press conference asking one of the questions: 'Is the case definitely solved?'

241

The spokesman's face appeared on the screen again, in medium close-up.

'We're still talking to his relatives and friends,' he said, 'but in short order the answer to your question is: Yes, we think so. He'd told several people he'd intended to kill the Vice President, and there were the letters. No-one took him very seriously, unfortunately, because he was a rather unbalanced person. But it looks as though — as he told the *Post* — Mr. Liversedge's elevation to the presidency was what triggered him into doing it. We're still checking into how he got hold of the weapon, a small missile-launcher of German design, but he was in the national reserve. I may add that he fits the description of a man seen leaving the scene of the assassination at the time.'

The station reporter's face came on again. He was explaining that this was the first that had been said about an eyewitness seeing a man. The police had kept this quiet, the reporter said, to help their investigation.

There followed an interview with a leader of the NAACP, expressing his outrage at the killing, his satisfaction at knowing that the case was apparently solved.

The face of the weekend anchor, a woman, came on, saying: 'Coming up — an upset at Wimbledon.' Muir switched off the television. The radio was giving a longer version of the spokesman's answers to questions — the name of the motel, of Flug's wife, and other details. Muir wondered if Wong had caught the news. One person who had was Adelaide, whose call came through almost at once.

'I presume you've heard,' she said succinctly.

'Yes.'

'He sounds like a tacky little man.' She paused. 'What a waste — he even went home to Alabama and killed himself. Well, I guess it doesn't make any difference now, who did it, does it?'

'At least it puts the matter to rest,' he heard himself saying glibly.

'That's true. A long investigation would have been searing, I think. To tell you the truth, I'll be glad when Thursday's over and I can go home. Although I must say the press has been very proper, very considerate.'

'That's good. If there's anything you need, just let me know.'

'Most kind, Donald.' He heard her put the receiver down.

About thirty minutes later, Muir was back at his desk writing when Raines called again.

'Don, I'm terribly sorry, I just asked if you were warned about the press conference, and I find you weren't.'

'It doesn't matter. There'll be a blow-by-blow in the *Post* tomorrow.'

'But you probably wanted to ask some questions. I'm awfully sorry.'

'I'm not on the usual list for your press people,' Muir explained. 'I only cover Justice very occasionally. I don't think I've ever spoken to Cunningham,' he added, naming the spokesman who had just been on screen.

'The thing broke just after I left the office, not long after I spoke to you,' Raines said. 'After I came back here, I was terribly busy.'

Muir thought: If you only knew how little I want to know about the false confession of Leroy Flug.

Raines went on: 'Anyway, I'll do all I can to help. Because of the book, I guess it's really more important for you than for any of your colleagues.'

'That's true,' said Muir. He reflected that if they were all convinced that Flug was the guilty party, and if he wasn't going to doubt that conviction in his book, he would have to muster some professional zeal for the Flug solution.

'I'll be hearing from you, Don,' said Raines.

'Right. I'll be calling you, Jack,' said Muir.

As he put the receiver down, he thought about Raines' exaggerated apologies, his almost effusive offers of further help. That sort of attitude was not usual at the FBI, even from a friendly source. Raines was obviously *feeling good*. The whole cop establishment must be feeling better, Muir thought, now that the case was solved — and without the necessity for a trial. If they never found out how

Flug got hold of the weapon — and they obviously couldn't, since he had never gotten hold of it — it wouldn't matter, he guessed. When had they ever cleared up a presidential assassination case completely? Flug had had to kill himself to avoid being questioned — to avoid the FBI finding out that he wasn't guilty.

Vuissane broke into his thoughts.

'It's past seven. Do you still want to go to the Dufresnes'?'

Dufresne was the cultural counselor at the French embassy. He was independently wealthy, and he and his wife entertained frequently in their Georgetown house. It would be a welcome distraction for both Vuissane and himself, Muir thought, and her question seemed to confirm that that was how she felt.

'Why not?' he said affirmatively.

* * *

The house, large by Georgetown standards but small by Dufresne's, was, as usual, overcrowded. Through a window, Muir could see that the tiny yard was awash in people of several nationalities, and the two downstairs reception rooms were heavy with smoke and voices. Muir paused to exchange amenities with a television producer who was flattering an ex-senator into liquored volubility, and Vuissane found a senior Belgian diplomat who had been at the Liversedge soirée at which she had sung. Muir took a vodka-tonic from a tray offered by a hired waiter and went out into the yard. By a clump of flowering bushes, a white-haired figure was holding forth to a rapt audience which was composed of a former secretary of state, a woman from the National Endowment for the Humanities and two men reporters.

Judge Edward Mulvany had, for many years, enjoyed an undistinguished term on the District of Columbia bench, noted mostly for the severity of his sentencing. He had been reversed often, both on sentencing and procedure. Then he had tried a noted Watergate case, nearly a decade before, and become a figure of legend. He had written his book, and retired in glory. No-one remembered that the Watergate case had been almost the only one where he hadn't goofed, and he enjoyed his new role on the Georgetown circuit as a sort of Oliver Wendell Holmes for the common man.

'You don't need to know how he got hold of the weapon in a case like this,' he was explaining, in a tone that brooked no contradiction. 'Obviously a weapon was used, but we have a confession that does not say what the weapon was. To doubt Flug, you would have had to find him an alibi, without his cooperation. In any event, no judicial action is necessary, unless such an alibi is produced and proven.'

'The chances were never strong that Liversedge was killed for any reason but his color.' The new voice was Ray Fielding, a Washington investigative reporter for the New York *Times*. 'The notion that the South African government would plot to kill — would kill — a president of the United States was as unlikely as to think that the Russians would do it.'

The woman from the Endowment agreed. 'Presidents are murdered by kooks, not coldblooded planners, at least in this country. There's never been a *coup d'état*. Presidential assassinations have always been a statement.'

'A sort of heavy vote of no-confidence from an individual,' said the former secretary of state. His tired, pink features bore the traces of a cherubic grin.

'The black crowd at the *Post* will go to jail simply for pretending to have done it,' said the other reporter. 'There's bound to be a tiny suspicion of doubt about Flug's confession because he never stood trial.'

'No, I can understand his reasoning,' piped Judge Mulvany. 'Imprisonment in cases like that is pretty awful. Lights on all the time, guards watching you night and day, no contact with other prisoners. The brief courtroom ordeal. Then, all sorts of appeals — judicial, clemency. Then, the chair. He did the inevitable — he executed himself. Machismo — no question of being handcuffed, booed, humiliated. If I'd known that it was Flug, I think I would have predicted suicide.'

'I'm sorry, though, that you, or rather one of your successors, didn't get a chance to put him in court, Ed,' said former Secretary Rohrbach. 'Even with a guilty plea, and no actual trial, it would have been an historic moment. And, who knows, if he had been arrested, he might have pled innocent and invented some explanation for his confession.'

'I can't see how anyone could doubt he did it,' said Fielding. 'The feds were convinced from the start that it was a racist thing.'

The wife of a British diplomat had just joined the group. She said: 'What do you think about it all, Don? You knew the Vice President so well.'

'My maid told me it was a Nazi or a Kluxer,' said Muir. 'She reads fortunes and she's usually a step ahead of the feds in matters of this sort.'

'My maid reads fortunes too,' said Judge Mulvany, his weathered gaze relaxing. 'She told me on Friday that the murderer was a South African. I'm going to tell her tomorrow that she was close.'

'I'd still liked to have talked to the guy,'

said the other reporter.

'Fat chance, once he was arrested,' said Fielding. 'But he would have made a good subject on *Face the Nation*.'

'We've never had an assassination of this sort in the United Kingdom,' said the British diplomat's wife. The remark sounded smug, but Muir guessed it was her accent that made it sound that way. 'But if we had a black prime minister, someone would probably try, I'm afraid.'

'When you think about it,' said Rohrbach, 'we've never had an assassination that wasn't completely domestic. I remember thinking that, when the papers were speculating on lobby groups. Even the South Africans, who would have been the most disturbed by Liversedge becoming President, wouldn't take a decision like that, as Ray says.'

'They've killed some people in this country,' Fielding said. 'I knew that for a fact, even before today's news briefing.' Muir wondered who his source was. Did he share Raines with Fielding? 'But they were all South African citizens,' Fielding added.

'That's my point,' said Rohrbach. 'Assassinations are virtually always domestic political affairs. We didn't kill President Diem — the Viets did it themselves. Kennedy didn't mind seeing him go, and our people were informed of the plotting, but the decision was theirs.'

'It's all so ugly,' said the Englishwoman. 'Agatha Christie was so much more civilized. It was usually the butler who did it.'

'It certainly wasn't the butler who killed Roger Liversedge, my dear,' Mulvany said. He won a chorus of approving chuckles.

Part Three

Sign-Off

1

Muir awoke on Monday morning feeling unusually rested. He had had no dream — no telephone was ringing. Vuissane still slept, soundly. They were in his apartment. He made coffee and took the papers and the typescript of the book to the terrace. He spent only five minutes on the *Post*. He knew he had a bestseller, and he felt good about that. He would even finish on time for Carl's insistent deadline. He had everything in the book now, except Vuissane with Roberts, and Wong Hwan's final service to the President and his adopted country. The two most important points about Roger's death were missing, the Flug ending was untrue, but the book was fine. Muir reflected that his own discretion, in its way, was even less excusable than Wong Hwan's distracted gesture. Muir was not omitting what he knew from concern for the nation, or for Ellen Roberts, or for

Hank Roberts' memory, but only out of concern for Vuissane — and a strange empathy for Hwan, with his misguided view of loyalty to Roberts. But after all, Muir tried to reassure himself again, Hwan had never confessed to anything. It was only his, Muir's, conclusion, however sure he was of it.

The hardest thing to write was his 'acceptance' of the official view: The little man he had seen fleeing from the scene had to be diminutive Leroy Flug, the poor, obsessional racist who had now gotten his name into the history books because of a murder which he would probably never really have dared to do, or even known how to plan. Muir wondered if Flug wasn't really the only winner in all of this: His friends would be saying 'Jeez! Leroy! He really did it!'

But Roger, too, had gained in a way. He would probably not have been a very good president, and he would have had no influence for getting through legislation in the way Tony Gentiluomo would, for a while. He would probably not have enjoyed being president, even. But now, at last, he had become a figure whom nearly all Americans could respect: a martyr. Yet really, Muir thought guiltily, the main winner was himself, because he was alive to enjoy the spoils. Just thinking of the movie rights made him feel a tinge of euphoria.

The first call of the morning was from Mike O'Donnell.

'Don't do any articles without them contacting me,' Mike said. 'Them' clearly meant editors. 'We'll set a minimum at ten thousand dollars.'

'Talk to Carl,' said Muir. 'He may want some things held till the book comes out.'

'Will do,' said Mike.

It was eight-thirty. Muir called the front desk and asked them to take all calls until four o'clock. He would give the day over to the book.

* * *

But as he sat down to write, the immensity of his deception suddenly overwhelmed him. Vuissane still slept, and he could hear nothing but his own insistent thoughts in the silent room. Could he really deceive everybody in this way? What ethical arguments could there possibly be for going along with the Flug caper? Perhaps, after all, he told himself, he should tell the truth. The book would still be a bestseller, and he and Vuissane could go away. They could go to France. They could marry, which would solve the problem of her immigration status, if they ever wanted to return. He would obviously have to talk with her.

To talk with her. Contemplating that, he knew at once that his idea was a non-starter. For the rest of her life, she would be known for only one thing. That would be bad enough for a bookkeeper or a sales assistant, but it would be a great deal worse for someone in the public eye. He knew she was far too sensitive to survive the notoriety. As things stood, the whole episode was, for Vuissane, just a horrible, innocent accident: President Roberts' heart condition would have carried him off, weeks or months or a few years later, in any event. She did not know that she had indirectly caused

Liversedge's murder also, as part of a cover-up which benefitted her. She thought Liversedge's death was the work of Flug and the Ku Klux Klan. Adding the truth about that to her conscience — and publishing it — was unthinkable.

There had to be a solution that could spare Vuissane, and close the case that everyone now seemed satisfied was closed anyway, and still spare his own conscience. He could think of only one solution.

He reached for a sheet of his printed notepaper and rolled it into his typewriter.

'Dear Carl,' he began, 'I have given the book a lot of thought in the past few days.' He paused briefly, then typed on: 'Needless to say, Roger's death has affected me personally, perhaps more than I can say. Although a book showing Roger with all his warts was something I could have done while he was alive, it seems more and more like a thing I couldn't do to his memory.'

He pulled the page out and rolled it into a ball. Carl would want to argue with him. What were the warts? He would want to read the passages. There weren't that many warts, after all. Carl would argue that Muir could rewrite those parts, and let Liversedge down more lightly. And what were warts? His impotence, for instance, would now attract more sympathy than scorn. He tried again to compose a letter to his editor.

'Dear Carl,' he typed, 'Since the assassination I have learned a number of troublesome facts that make it emotionally and morally impossible for me to write the Liversedge book at all. I know this will come as a great shock to you, but — '

He pulled the sheet from the machine. My God, what a can of worms a letter like that would stir up! He walked to the bathroom, tore the page into pieces and flushed it down the toilet. Then, he wished he had burned it instead, for greater security.

He walked out onto the terrace, anxious to hear the sounds of life outside his own. But the notion of writing a book that contained a monstrous lie still remained unsolved. How could *any* serious reporter do such a thing? Even if the lie was never exposed, and it probably never would be, it would haunt him for the rest of his days. A cover-up! — to a reporter, it sounded as bad as assassination itself.

Yet how could he *not* write it, without raising a forest of questions? Failing to write the book was perhaps the only way that he could provoke others into raking the embers of the case, perhaps ensuring that everything which he wanted to conceal would become public knowledge — at the hands of some other reporter. And after all, he thought again, there was always the money — a hard-cover sale beyond his wildest dreams, the paperback all over the supermarkets as well as the bookstores, the foreign rights in every imaginable language, the film. There was no way that he was not going to clear seven figures. Muir recalled Somerset Maugham saying that money was a sixth sense without which you could not properly appreciate the other five. Money would, in this case, be a compensation for an ethic discarded, a professional disgrace committed. And it would keep Vuissane safe — at least he would be doing one thing right.

He put a fresh, blank sheet of paper in the machine and swiftly typed the words: 'Chapter Thirteen'.

★ ★ ★

That afternoon, Adelaide called.

'Donald, do you remember Lesley Twine?'

'She's the pastor of the Unitarian church of which your father used to be minister,' Muir said.

'Right. She's in Washington for Roger's rites. She got in last night: She's staying here at the hotel. We had breakfast at the White House this morning with President Gentiluomo. It was interesting.' There seemed an unexpected note in her voice. Mirth? 'Would you like to talk to her again? She says you visited Queenston in the spring.'

'Yes. Would you like to come round here — now?'

A few minutes later, they were at the door. Twine was a middle-aged, motherly figure. Except for her shapeless summer dress, she looked, Muir thought, like a good-natured nun.

They sat on the terrace and drank iced tea. Adelaide said: 'Archbishop Llewellyn and Mrs. Roberts were there. It was a breakfast to discuss the funeral arrangements. And d'you know what? The President thought that Unitarians were Christians!'

'He thought we were just another Protestant sect,' said Twine. 'Of course, I suppose I shouldn't be surprised; the Catholics aren't strong on comparative religion. I let Archbishop Llewellyn explain why we were called Unitarian-Universalists. He told the President about our rejection of the Messiah concept. He said we were closer to the Muslims than to the Jews or the Christians, and closer still to the American Indians. The President seemed startled. But when the Archbishop got to the Universalist bit, he seemed even more disturbed.'

'Yes, he said,' Adelaide began, and now

she was actually smiling as she imitated a man's voice, ' 'I never dreamed Roger was anything like that.' ' She grinned at Twine.

'I was a bit puzzled myself at the notion of a double funeral,' said Muir. 'Did Gentiluomo really plan for a single Protestant ceremony?'

'He wanted me to serve as a sort of acolyte to the Archbishop,' said Twine. 'I could have ended up carrying a crucifix, perhaps waving an instrument of torture over the crowds.'

'You should mention this in the book,' said Adelaide. 'It will amuse Roger when he gets his review copy for the *Celestial Times*.'

'I shall,' said Muir. 'So, what did you decide?'

'Well, I only met Mr. Liversedge once, when he was Governor,' said Twine. 'He came to the church, and it was a sort of political occasion, the hometown bit. It would have been vulgar to discuss religion, and we didn't. But there are so many different views among Unitarians, so I thought I'd better ask Miss

Liversedge what sort of a Unitarian he was.'

'And I had to say,' Adelaide broke in, 'that the last time I remember him discussing religion at all was thirty years ago. That was after Korea, when he was telling me about Janet. You'll remember she was a Christian convert who'd gone back to Buddhism.' She paused. 'Did he ever discuss religion with you, for the book?'

'Yes, once,' said Muir. 'In Korea, he was very much taken with Buddhism, and we'd discussed that, a few times, in the past. Before his first trip to the Middle East, he read the Koran, and he was surprised to learn that it wasn't required reading for United States diplomats in the area.' He looked at Twine. 'I suppose you could say he was a Universalist, in your terms. He respected all religions, including non-Unitarian, that is non-monotheist, ones, like Buddhism — beliefs which involve no god at all.'

'Agnostic?' asked Twine.

'I would say so.'

'And what are you, if I may ask?'

265

'I think I'm a lapsed Zen Buddhist,' said Muir, smiling.

'What lapsed you?'

'My job.'

Twine nodded, and looked at Adelaide. 'Well, I believe I know best how to handle this, now. I'll call the Archbishop when we get back to the hotel.'

'He was very nice, the Archbishop,' said Adelaide. 'He wore a Brooks Brothers suit. He reminded me a bit of Daddy, in a way, except for — uh — uh' Muir assumed that she was going to mention Llewellyn's white skin, but he should have known Adelaide better — 'except for the clerical collar,' she concluded.

*　★　★*

Not long after they left, Mike O'Donnell called.

'I've talked to Carl. We agree that the first priority is to finish the book this week. But I've tentatively accepted a couple of things, if you agree.' One was for Muir to write an article of recollections of Liversedge for *The New York*

Times Magazine. Another was to appear on one of the serious talk shows; and there was some sort of advisory role on a network special. The payments that Mike had obtained all sounded unusually generous.

Back in the studio that night, it seemed as if a small eternity had passed since Friday. Muir talked some more about Liversedge. He didn't mention Flug; he didn't want to carry deceit any further than was necessary. It was bad enough having to mention Flug in the book, and he supposed that he would be cited in some report as a witness to the fleeing figure, the man whose face he hadn't seen. After all, he reminded himself again, even Vuissane believed that Flug was the assassin. Maybe Flug had believed it, in the end.

He talked of the funeral ceremonies that would take place at Arlington Memorial Cemetery on Thursday, by which time heads of state would have flown in from all over the world. With Flug's confession and suicide, and the funeral plans, the story was dying. The

UPI ticker was already mentioning President Gentiluomo more than his predecessors. There was even the first Gentiluomo joke going the rounds in Washington — that the old Italian pol hadn't taken the oath, but the Fifth Amendment.

Muir played 'Solitaire' again, explaining that 'that great and good French singer, Vuissane, has produced a version of her own, in French, which I heard on Saturday night at Rufus' and which I hope more of you will be able to hear. Meanwhile, here's Ginger Ford once more. With my love, Vuissane.' No listener would suspect that he meant that seriously, except Vuissane and a few of their friends.

As he sat back, he wondered why Vuissane and he were communicating in a song that talked of solitude. He couldn't think of an answer. Largely to revive his own spirits, he decided it was time to go back to humor.

He announced the end of the garbage-collectors' strike in Calcutta, which he had noticed in the evening paper, and then he added: 'You all remember, I guess, the story that gave its name to shaggy-dog stories? — about the man who lost a shaggy dog and searched for it all over the world. But none of the dogs that people found for him were ever as shaggy as the dog he had lost. Until finally someone found a dog so shaggy it was almost unbelievable, and the man said: 'Oh no, not *that* shaggy.'

'Well, did you know where the first sick joke came from? It came, like the news of that garbage-collectors' strike, from India.

'Seems there was this youth called Chandra whose father had betrothed him to the daughter of a distant friend. Finally, the time came for the two young people to meet. And Chandra discovered that Laxmi was the ugliest girl he had ever seen. She was so ugly, he threw up. Every time Chandra saw Laxmi, he threw up. He was so worried at the thought that he must marry her that he got ulcers. So they took him to hospital and the surgeon said: 'Before I can operate on you, you must clear your digestive system. You will eat nothing for twenty-four hours.' When

Laxmi came to see Chandra at the hospital on the night before the operation, Chandra was starving and he couldn't throw up. And Laxmi burst into tears and said: 'What's the matter, Chandra? Don't you love me any more?'

'That, folks, was the first sick joke,' Muir said. Then he found himself thinking of Vuissane and Hwan and Flug — the sick joke on everyone which he could not tell.

When Art Foster appeared a few moments before midnight, they engaged in the usual 'transfer' dialogue.

'Did you have a good day, Art?' Muir asked.

'Pretty good. How about you?'

'No complaints,' said Muir. Then he went into his usual sign-off routine.

He thought of Mrs. No-Name out there, presumably listening. Would she call him again, now? He hoped not. He didn't want to see her again. He had enough problems of his own, without accommodating hers. He wished he hadn't used the code words. She had said that his brief encounter with her would be memorable, but memorable experiences should not be repeated. If they saw each other more, they might end up by knowing each other. Right now, he was beginning to question whether he knew himself.

But perversely, he was thinking of Mrs. No-Name that night as he made love to Vuissane.

★ ★ ★

In his dream, Vuissane and Mrs. No-Name were talking at a party. He joined them, and Vuissane said: 'Why didn't you tell me about Margie before? She's adorable.' Mrs. No-Name was moving nearer to him with her blood-red lips and she put her hand behind his back to keep him close. Vuissane only laughed at the gesture. 'He's mine!' Vuissane said, smiling, and she began to take off her dress, in the rapid and abandoned way that Mrs. No-Name had done at the hotel. From another room, a man was calling: 'Will somebody get that goddam phone?'

271

It wasn't the phone. It was the doorbell. Liberty was standing there, and it seemed that she was trying to read all four papers' front pages at once. Muir reflected that cereal boxes would never seem as interesting again.

'Din' I tell ya? It were a cracker from Alabama!'

In the kitchen, she said: 'You wan' me to make that strong coffee?' He nodded. They sat down to their usual cereal breakfast, but Muir felt distracted. Liberty's homespun wisdom was based, today, on a great deception, and everything she said about Flug reminded Muir of his own deceit. After listening to her for a while, and responding in monosyllables, he took his coffee on to the terrace. He was out there, reading the *Post*, when Liberty appeared again.

'There's a nice young man at the door who wanna see you. He say you know him.'

Although she didn't say that the caller was black — Liberty usually distinguished everybody according to their color or probable ethnic origin — he guessed it was Jacks.

'Bring him out.'

He heard her asking the caller if he would like coffee, and saying: 'You won't like the strong sort Mister Muir drinks.'

Muir made room for Jacks on the foot of the lounger. Jacks was carrying his own copy of the *Post*.

'You see this jive? That wasn't no Flug. Flug jus' a crazy pretendin' he did it. Look at the picture,' Jacks said.

A poor snapshot, much enlarged, showed Flug as short but rather chunky.

'The man I see was, well, kinda fine. He wasn't no guy like that. The face is wrong.'

'You said you only saw the butt, getting in the taxi, and when you last saw him he was a block away, and it was night.'

'Well, I think about it, and I did see a little of him as he run away, down by the river. He look sorta oriental.'

'It was dark, and you were high, remember. When the choppers arrived, you thought for a moment you were still in Nam. Memories play tricks.'

'That ain't the face,' said Jacks,

pointing again at Flug's picture in the *Post*.

'How can you be sure?' asked Muir. 'Everything else adds up — his past, his letters to Liversedge, his boasts to friends that he was going to kill him. He'd been staying in Georgetown until the morning after the murder. He was in the national reserve — that's probably how he got the weapon.'

Jacks still looked dissatisfied.

'I'd swear on a stack of Bibles that ain't him.'

'Where?'

Liberty appeared with some ordinary American coffee for Jacks to drink. When she had gone, Jacks said: 'You know I can't talk to no-one. Not with that parole jive, man. Wouldn't do no good, no how. Liversedge dead. Yet I know — '

'You'll never be sure,' Muir said.

But by the time Jacks left, ten minutes later, he felt he had only half-convinced him. Still, he reflected, in Jacks' case, that was enough.

Shortly after the door closed on the

visitor, Liberty came out on the terrace again.

'Miss Wishing stirring,' she reported. She stayed there, looking wistfully at the peaceful river.

'He were handsome, that boy,' she said. 'He remin' me of my first beau.'

Shapeless and jowled, Liberty was the sort of woman of whom people would carelessly say that it was impossible to imagine that she had ever been goodlooking. But Muir was a journalist, and journalists knew that there was really nothing that it was impossible to believe. She had had a beau, back there in Pittsburgh, long ago, and of course others: She had been married.

'I 'member how he come to my house for that first date. I were fourteen and he were sixteen.'

'Don't tell me,' Muir said, 'and your son was three.'

Liberty gave a hoarse, loud laugh that startled the ducks near Thompson's Boatyard into flight. She put the palms of her hands on her thighs and walked backward, in a sort of involuntary motion, shaking with glottal mirth.

'Mister Muir, you a real card.' She repeated what he had said, twice.

He was back to reading the paper when she began again: 'He come to the house because it were my first date, an' my father wanna look him over. I 'member, he were goodlookin', jus' like that boy, an' he speak nice. He say things other boys wouldn't say. I 'member, he stand on the stoop an' look in at us all, and he say 'The love of Liberty brought me here.' ' She laughed again, and the laugh seemed to go right up her nostrils, like a sneeze.

★　★　★

Adelaide called again in the afternoon. After they had exchanged amenities, Muir said: 'Did Lesley Twine set everything up with the Archbishop?'

'Yes, that's all arranged, I think. Now, there's something else, Donald. The President called me today and he asked how many members of Roger's family were here. I explained that we were the only children, and that of course we had no children of our own, no nieces or nephews. Most of our cousins are far away. The only one who was a real friend of Roger's, Archie, is on Guam. Only one cousin wanted to come — Willie, in New York, but I discouraged him. He's rather disreputable, and I know he only wanted to come to have his picture taken with the President. So I told the President there was only me, and of course Roger's staff, from our side, and I asked if I could bring an old family friend along.'

Muir smiled at the expression 'from our side'. She was making it sound like a wedding.

'I mean you, of course,' said Adelaide. 'Would your friend — I didn't catch her name — like to come as well?'

'No, I don't think so. She doesn't like funerals.'

'I understand,' said Adelaide. Oh no you don't, thought Muir.

'So you'll be with me, will you?'

'Of course. I'd like that, very much.'

2

There were some light showers, Thursday morning. Liberty was soaking wet when she arrived, and was soon walking around in her underwear and Muir's bathrobe. From the terrace, after breakfast, he could see the old plantation house, across the river, on the hill: The rest of Arlington Memorial Cemetery was concealed behind trees. He had already rewritten the start of the book to begin with the assassination, but now he decided to change it again and begin with the funeral. He would end, instead — and as succinctly as possible — on the explosion. That way, perhaps he could avoid mentioning the investigation, or Flug, at all.

The black limousine from the General Services Administration came by at ten-fifteen. It had stopped raining by then, but the sky was still overcast. His fellow-passengers, Len Duval and Len's wife Marie, were already inside the car. They had been picked up from their home in Chevy Chase. Duval had been an editorialist with the Providence *Journal* before joining Roger as the Vice President's press secretary. He would be going back to the paper, now. He and Marie were part of Rhode Island's large French-Canadian community. They had only been married for a year. Marie was very young, just out of college, but her black veil made her look ten years older.

'I suppose you heard about the complications with the ceremony,' said Duval. 'I'm a Roman Catholic too; I wouldn't have been any wiser than the President.'

'I gather they've settled all that,' said Muir.

The serious-faced chauffeur drove the single block to the Rock Creek Parkway, turned left, ignoring the interdiction sign, and drove past the Kennedy Center. He stopped on the ramp leading up to the Lincoln Memorial. Some other limousines were already waiting there. Duval looked at his watch.

'I figure we've got nearly thirty minutes of this,' he said.

Normally, Muir and Duval enjoyed talking together, but now a dialogue seemed difficult. It was not just the continual thinking about Roger and how he had died; the whole mystique of a presidential funeral was getting to them. Marie's black veil had done it, Muir thought.

After about ten minutes, Duval tried to make normal conversation. He said: 'If I'd known we were going to lose Roger so soon, I'd have decided to write a book myself.'

'There's room for at least two,' said Muir, encouragingly.

'Maybe Wong Hwan will write his memoirs — 'My Two Presidents',' said Duval, smiling.

'His English is a bit wobbly,' said Muir.

'Duke Fain would ghost it for him. He's ghosted everybody.'

Conversation lapsed again, to resume only intermittently. At one point, Muir heard himself saying: 'Roger despised funerals. He thought they were a waste of money. I wonder what he'd make of his own.'

'That's right, he did,' Duval said. Marie still sat silently; she had taken a rosary from her purse and was using it, mumbling mutely to herself.

'He told me about one of his uncles, Uncle Jerry, in San Francisco,' Muir said. 'Uncle Jerry was very ill and he couldn't afford treatment and he died at home. There wasn't any money for the funeral, but his neighbors and friends collected two thousand dollars and gave him a fine send-off. Roger said that if Uncle Jerry had asked for two thousand dollars to get him into hospital, they wouldn't have come up with two hundred.'

'He had a point,' Duval said.

Finally, it was clear from a movement in the crowds around the Memorial, a sudden semi-hush, that the cortege was arriving from the Mall.

There were two riderless horses this time, two gun-carriages carrying the flag-draped caskets, moving side by side on to the bridge. The President's car came next. Gentiluomo was sitting with

Mrs. Roberts on the back seat. Mrs. Gentiluomo was sitting on the bench seat, behind the driver, with Adelaide. The cars with the rest of the Roberts family — children, spouses, their children — followed. Then came the cars with the visiting heads of state and government, then the president pro-tem of the Senate, the acting Speaker of the House, the cabinet officers, other foreign visitors, the ambassadors, the chiefs of staff. After a while, you could only guess at what the protocular order was meant to be. Duval had been right: It was at least half an hour before their own driver charged his engine.

'We're running late,' said Duval. He was, for a moment, a press secretary again.

It seemed an eternity, crossing the bridge, rounding the traffic circle, then driving up the hill into the cemetery itself, past endless markers.

'You're sitting behind Miss Liversedge, I understand,' said Duval. Muir wondered vaguely how that would be arranged.

When they came to a halt, a Marine

private in dress uniform opened the door. Marie got out, then Duval. Muir shuffled over the seat to follow. A Marine sergeant looked at the number on the windshield and walked over quickly.

'Mr. Muir?' he asked Duval.

'That's Mr. Muir.'

'Please follow me, sir,' said the sergeant.

Muir was shown to a chair in the second row, at the graveside. The front row and most of the second was empty. The principals, Muir realized, must all be inside the chapel. Roger's caisson was standing in the open, its casket still aboard. Roberts' caisson was nearby, empty. The casket would be inside the chapel, where the Archbishop would be doing his act. Muir looked at the reporters' enclosure, recognizing faces. Photographers and cameramen were in a separate enclosure, chatting quietly among themselves.

It began to rain slightly again, but no-one seemed to notice. Nearly all of the women were wearing hats. A few wore veils, and drips of water began to appear on these. It seemed an unconscionably long time before the Marines emerged from the chapel, carrying Roberts down the steps. President and Mrs. Gentiluomo appeared with Adelaide and the Roberts family. About a hundred more people followed. Other Marines began to lift Roger's casket from the caisson. By some deft drill, both caskets arrived at the two adjoining grave-sites at the same moment. The photographers and television cameramen were busy. The front rows of chairs began to fill up. More photographs. Reeves and Packer were watching to make sure that none of the photographers came closer than the agreed distance.

Adelaide, in her black chiffon, took her seat in front of Muir, on Gentiluomo's left. Ellen Roberts was on his right. Adelaide was not veiled, and seemed composed. Gentiluomo looked haggard. His eyes were red, as though he had been crying. Muir noted that there was dandruff on one presidential shoulder. Ellen Roberts was sniffing, raising her veil to slip in a white lace handkerchief. Adelaide looked over her left shoulder at

Muir, making a little sign with a gloved right hand.

'So glad you could come,' she said. She made it sound like a garden party. Muir patted her hand and nodded. The ambiance was getting to him. He thought: Maybe they should have left Roger in the river.

Archbishop Llewellyn looked magnificent in his robes, surrounded by an attendant black priest and several acolytes. His craggy features, under thinning, wavy gray hair, looked like an actor's.

Lesley Twine had appeared from somewhere, and waited, alone, with Roger's casket and Roger's attendant Marines.

The Episcopal ceremony went first. Soon, everybody's head was bent in prayer, or in reminiscence. The heads rose again. The Archbishop read from the Book. The final act was approaching.

'Dust unto dust, ashes unto ashes,' Llewellyn was intoning in his archiepiscopal tenor. Taut Marines were lowering Roberts' heavy casket into the hole. It seemed like an anticlimax.

All heads were turned toward Lesley Twine. Except for the rather somber dark gray dress and the serious face, she looked like a den mother at summer camp about to announce that chow was ready. Muir was envisaging how she must have looked as a little girl. But the image disappeared as she spoke. Her voice was strong, meant to carry in the open air.

'We know not whence we came, or why, or the reason for our coming and going,' she said. 'We are not even sure if we have come or if we go.' She was speaking extemporaneously. 'Many have thought on this,' she said.

She quoted from the Koran. She even quoted from the Kama Sutra. She spoke of Gautama, who became the Buddha. She told the story of life as it is understood by the Rosebud Sioux. She spoke of the possibility of reincarnation. In about five minutes, she had said all that she wanted to say about life and death. She nodded to the warrant officer in charge of the burial detail, and the laying of a casket was reenacted. Muir found himself wondering if Flug had already been buried in some anonymous graveyard in Leander. He assumed that Wong Hwan was not there, at Arlington, and he wondered what pretext he had found for not attending — the need to prepare for the post-funeral reception of visiting foreign dignitaries, at the White House?

Muir began to shift in his seat, feeling restless. Adelaide turned to say something to him. Then the ceremonial cannons began to boom, and he missed her words. It was something about Roger's wrist-watch. He supposed they had recovered it, and she wanted to give it to him.

'I said — ' she began again, to be cut off by another round of ceremonial fire.

'Tell you later,' she said quickly, between volleys. He nodded. Adelaide would have to go to the White House, and stand in the receiving line. He would see her in the afternoon. It was time, he thought, to do that *New York Times Magazine* piece, and to finish the book. His bestseller. That was the only thing that he could do for Adelaide, or Roger. And himself.

We do hope that you have enjoyed reading this large print book.

Did you know that all of our titles are available for purchase?

We publish a wide range of high quality large print books including:
Romances, Mysteries, Classics
General Fiction
Non Fiction and Westerns

Special interest titles available in large print are:
The Little Oxford Dictionary
Music Book, Song Book
Hymn Book, Service Book

Also available from us courtesy of Oxford University Press:
Young Readers' Dictionary
(large print edition)
Young Readers' Thesaurus
(large print edition)

For further information or a free brochure, please contact us at:
Ulverscroft Large Print Books Ltd.,
The Green, Bradgate Road, Anstey,
Leicester, LE7 7FU, England.
Tel: (00 44) **0116 236 4325**
Fax: (00 44) **0116 234 0205**

Other titles in the
Linford Mystery Library:

THAT INFERNAL TRIANGLE

Mark Ashton

An aeroplane goes down in the notorious Bermuda Triangle and on board is an Englishman recently heavily insured. The suspicious insurance company calls in Dan Felsen, former RAF pilot turned private investigator. Dan soon runs into trouble, which makes him suspect the infernal triangle is being used as a front for a much more sinister reason for the disappearance. His search for clues leads him to the Bahamas, the Caribbean and into a hurricane before he resolves the mystery.

THE GUILTY WITNESSES

John Newton Chance

Jonathan Blake had become involved in finding out just who had stolen a precious statuette. A gang of amateurs had so clever a plot that they had attracted the attention of a group of international spies, who habitually used amateurs as guide dogs to secret places of treasure and other things. Then, of course, the amateurs were disposed of. Jonathan Blake found himself being shot at because the guide dogs had lost their way . . .

THIS SIDE OF HELL

Robert Charles

Corporal David Canning buried his best friend below the burning African sand. Then he was alone, with a bullet-sprayed ambulance containing five seriously injured men and one hysterical nurse in his care. He faced heat, dust, thirst and hunger; and somewhere in the area roamed almost two hundred blood-crazed tribesmen led by a white mercenary with his own desperate reasons for catching up with the sole survivors of the massacre. But Canning vowed that he would win through to safety.

HEAVY IRON

Basil Copper

In this action-packed adventure, Mike Faraday, the laconic L.A. private investigator, stumbles by accident into one of his most bizarre and lethal cases when he is asked to collect a fifty thousand dollar debt by wealthy club owner, Manny Richter. Instead, Mike becomes involved in a murderous web of death, crime and corruption until the solution is revealed in the most unexpected manner.

ICE IN THE SUN

Douglas Enefer

It seemed like the simplest of assignments when the Princess Petra di Maurentis flew into London from her island in the sun — but anything private eye Dale Shand takes on invariably turns out to be vastly different from what it seems. Like the alluring Princess herself, whose only character flaw is a tendency to steal anything not actually nailed to the floor. Dale is in it deep, mixed-up with the most colourful bunch of fakes even he has ever run up against . . .

THE DRUGS FARM

P. A. Foxall

The police suspect an American hard-line drugs dealer escaped from custody to be in England and they know of the expensively organised release from a maximum security prison of an industrial chemist. Their investigations are hampered by their sheer innocence of the criminals' resources and capacity for corruption, even in the citadel of power. No wonder there seems little chance of uncovering the criminals' product — a dangerous and hallucinogenic drug — that could threaten the young everywhere.